A NOTE ON THE AUTHOR

ELIZA ROBERTSON attended the University of Victoria and the University of East Anglia, where she received the 2011 Man Booker Scholarship. In 2013, she won the Commonwealth Short Story Prize and was a finalist for the CBC Short Story Prize and the Journey Prize. Her first story collection, *Wallflowers*, was shortlisted for the East Anglian Book Award and selected as a *New York Times* Editor's Choice. In 2015, she was named one of five emerging writers for the Writers' Trust of Canada's Five x Five program and in 2017 she won the *Australian Book Review* Elizabeth Jolley Prize. She lives in Montreal.

elizarobertson.com
@ElizaRoberts0n

ALSO BY ELIZA ROBERTSON
Wallflowers

DEMI-GODS

ELIZA ROBERTSON

BLOOMSBURY PUBLISHING
LONDON · OXFORD · NEW YORK · NEW DELHI · SYDNEY

BLOOMSBURY PUBLISHING
Bloomsbury Publishing Plc
50 Bedford Square, London, WC1B 3DP, UK

BLOOMSBURY, BLOOMSBURY PUBLISHING and the Diana logo are
trademarks of Bloomsbury Publishing Plc

First published in 2017 in Toronto, Canada in Hamish Hamilton
hardcover by Penguin Canada
First published in Great Britain 2017
This edition published 2018

Cover and interior design by Kelly Hill
Cover art: 'Sun and Swim' (detail) by James Rieck;
(jellyfish) Natalia Varlamova/Shutterstock.com

A catalogue record for this book is available from the British Library.

ISBN: HB: 978-1-4088-9041-7; TPB: 978-1-4088-9040-0;
PB: 978-1-4088-9038-7; EBOOK: 978-1-4088-9039-4

2 4 6 8 10 9 7 5 3 1

Printed and bound in Great Britain by CPI Group (UK) Ltd, Croydon CR0 4YY

MIX
Paper from
responsible sources
FSC® C020471

To find out more about our authors and books visit www.bloomsbury.com
and sign up for our newsletters

For Mom and Jesse

In the golden age, we communed with gods.
A god could be hidden, barely contained,
inside the costumes of normal men.
Nothing was certain. How could you refuse
a beggar's request or a gambler's wager,
the bold advance of the boss's only daughter,
without fear of causing offence to a god?
You would say yes. In the golden age,
whatever was offered, you would say yes.

—FRANCES LEVISTON, "THE GOLDEN AGE"

THE

BEACH

HOUSE

We must have met the brothers in 1950, because USA had defeated England in the FIFA World Cup. They arrived with the sun in them, their bodies hard and tan like peanuts, eyes chlorine blue—even in the woods, my bedroom, the log where Patrick burned the moths with a magnifying glass. Kenneth was handsome except the bridge of his nose where his brother had thrown a dictionary at his face. The bump made his smile slope. I knew he and my sister loved each other when she made a daisy chain and he tucked it in the pocket of his shorts. I wondered if Patrick and I loved each other. He had carved cheeks, a hairless chest and floral lips, like he had been sucking on a sweet. He preferred secluded places to play: we swam by ourselves; we lay under my bed where I found it difficult to breathe. The moths made me cry later, but I didn't tell him to stop. Their khaki wings looked folded from rice paper. I imagined ten moths circling a candle to form a lantern. One antenna was crooked. The wings ignited like dog-eared pages in a book.

I have been thinking about memory as a space we dwell in. A dwelling. On the one hand, the word denotes a residence, the place we return to—a house, a warm doorway, a nest. On the other, dwelling indicates a process of reflection. A lingering.

Maybe both involve lingering.

1

1950
—

Salt Spring Island, British Columbia

ON THE FIRST MORNING, Kenneth slept in; Joan buttered toast soldiers for Luke in the kitchen; Patrick and I slurped cornflakes at the table. Mom's dollhouse had disappeared. Dad had built it for her when he designed the beach house, off the same blueprints, slicing every wall to scale. The dollhouse stood no more than twelve inches high, and Mom kept it on the nesting tables by the window. I loved it, because my dad had joined the pine with his hands, because Mom kept it after he left. Eugene hated it for the same reason. The real beach house too. He wanted to sell. He left his yacht in San Diego—they could sell that also. Use the money to demolish this pile of driftwood and build a nicer one, he would say. To which my mother would laugh: You couldn't build a fucking sandwich, Gene. Which made him hate the dollhouse even more.

So he was pleased when it disappeared. He couldn't smooth the smile from his mouth.

Maybe someone tossed it in the chuck where it belongs, he said, leaning against the kitchen counter—the ease of his stance undermined by how his fingers clamped the coffee cup.

That's where someone belongs, she said. Her kimono gaped over her underwear, which had collected the blue dye of a pillowcase in the wash. By contrast, he had dressed in suit trousers and a starched shirt, his sleeves cuffed around his forearms.

He opened his mouth to return something snide, but she swallowed whatever he said with a shoulder-racking, lung-scraping cough. Intentionally, I think. Eugene traced his finger around the lip of his coffee mug as he waited for the cough to end. When his fingernail dipped into the hot liquid, he lifted it to his mouth.

Patrick didn't tell me to follow him, but I understood he wanted me to. He slid through the French doors, away from their bickering, and meandered down the lawn, onto the dirt path that wound to the beach. Here, he dangled a whip of kelp at his side and slashed empty crab shells from the rock. I imagined the beach stones were lava and leapt from log to log to avoid melting my shins. I was nine years old, he was eleven. He didn't speak as we walked. By now Mom and Eugene would be hurling insults at each other, which I hated more than when they petted each other's hands. So I trailed after him, springing between logs, kneeling for balance if I landed an unsteady one, tiptoeing along the lip of a trunk that had been hollowed by lightning. Long ago, a blue rowboat had been dumped on the beach grass beside the fort, the turf grown over it now, as if trying to reclaim the wood. Instead of climbing inside the fort, Patrick stopped at the boat and dropped his pack.

Help me lift this, he said.

Rust etched over the gunwale like dry blood; prongs of grass wedged through a gap in the bottom planks.

Why do you want it?

He crouched and dug two hands under the stern of the boat. —Get the other side, he said.

I was scared to find what lived under there. Joan said there were water snakes and I imagined cords of them nesting under the hull. I didn't mind snakes if I couldn't see them, but worried they would shoot from the grass up my ankles.

I'm waiting.

It's not going to float, if that's what you're thinking.

He didn't reply. Finally I leaned forward and slid the smallest segments of my fingers under the gunwale. We pried the boat from the grass that had clamped around it. If I looked down, I would panic and fling my side of the boat, even if I saw only shadow or beach crabs, so I trained my eyes on Patrick opposite me, who lifted his end of the boat higher than I could. Together, we flipped it onto the keel. No snakes shook from the grass, but in a pocket of rubbery beach weed sat a clutch of two eggs. Each was no larger than the butt of my palm, the shells clay green, murmured with black splashes.

Patrick swooped down and pinched one between his finger and thumb. —You think it's hot enough to fry eggs on the rock?

Put that back.

Why?

It's a baby.

He opened his mouth and lay the egg on his tongue, kissed his lips around it. After a moment, he parted his teeth and pushed the wet egg back into his palm.

What will you do for me?

He closed his fist around the egg and started to squeeze.

I worried the scent of his sweat and saliva would scare the mother. The thought of these two green eggs abandoned under the rowboat with no mother's belly to warm them welled tears in my eyes. I didn't want him to see.

Stop that.

What will you do?

Just put them down.

He smiled. In a smooth motion, he tucked the egg back in the nest, wiped his hand on his jeans and nipped a crushed cigarette from his pocket. He massaged the paper to reshape it and struck a match on the rock.

Come on, he said, pulling on the cigarette with his girlish lip. —Let's go for a sail.

He dragged the grass-chewed, wind-rattled boat to the water. He pushed the bow into the seafoam. Liquid sucked through the gap in the bottom planks and the hull filled an inch.

You don't mind getting a little wet, do you? he asked and held the stern steady for me to climb in.

It'll sink.

You scared, then?

I trained my eyes on him to test if he was serious. He wore a white T-shirt stuffed into blue jeans, which he had rolled around his knees. With the cigarette hanging from his mouth, he looked like a hobo from the desert who hunted rattle-snakes and skinned them for boots. I stepped carefully into the boat and sat in the nearest wood seat. The hull sank deeper. He climbed in and pushed the boat from the shore with his forearms, perching opposite me on the middle bench. The hull filled with more water, but we managed to float, as if the salt pushed us up and down at the same time. The sea filled my socks, the cold unravelling a shock up my back.

I resolved to visit the eggs the next day for signs of the mother. I'd sit on them myself if I had to.

Patrick grabbed the two chipped paddles that hung from the oarlocks. —What are you waiting for? You have to bail.

He started to row. I folded my fingers together and scooped water with my hands.

My dad owns a boat, he said. Twenty times bigger than this one.

That's impossible.

He lets me sail it on my own.

You're fibbing.

What do you know?

Our vessel drifted, half-submerged, from the shore. We bobbed past the harbour light, toward the more open stretch of ocean that linked the islands. It was a warm day, the bay sluggish around us—vitamin green, unbroken by waves. I swam here often; from the harbour light I could still front-stroke to shore. After ten minutes, Patrick's rowing started to flag. No matter how vigorously he heaved the oars, or I pushed out water, we continued to droop into the sea. Finally, he steered us to a rocky point where the island tongued underwater and the boat could rest in its own shallow pool. I felt embarrassed for him. I unbuckled my Mary Janes and tipped out the water. If the leather dried with salt streaks, Eugene would take one of the shoes and bend me over his knee and whack my bum.

When I looked up, Patrick was watching me with a hooked smile. His jeans were drenched and the water had splashed up his shirt, the cotton slick to his stomach, an air bubble at his navel.

What? I said.

His stare flickered to the space beside me. I turned to find a ruddy, fifteen-inch jellyfish bumping over the sunken lip of the boat. I gasped and pressed myself to the opposite side. I heard a soft plashing and imagined the jelly wobbling at my waist, but I couldn't bring myself to look, and it might have been water shushing over the rocks. After a moment, I worried Patrick had stopped talking to stall me, the creature inching closer without my notice. I glanced down. At the same instant, the tide nudged the jelly over the lip of the boat. Its mass wafted toward my lap. The bell sprawled the water like an open wound, the net of stingers grazing my thighs. I could feel the weight of them above my trousers. A low howl built in my throat, but I was too scared to cry in case the movement drew it closer. Then I knew the jelly didn't sting my legs through the pedal pushers, because I could feel it now—my right forearm where the tentacles seared my wrist. That's when I leapt from the water and clambered the rocks to the bluff ten feet above, where I buckled and pressed my burning arm into the dry grass. The creature still crashed into my mind, and I imagined it enfolding me, tangling my arms in its lattice. Patrick climbed the bluff a few minutes later with a handful of wet sea lettuce. He took my wrist and pressed the weeds onto the sting, which had started to blister. The pressure of his hand and the cool plants relieved the burn for a moment, but soon it started all over.

You know what kind of jelly that was?

I ignored him, clutching his hand tighter to ease the pain and my shaking, the jagged breath in my chest.

Lion's mane, he said. The biggest species of jellyfish in the world. One specimen measured a hundred and thirty feet. Longer than a blue whale.

I tried not to listen to him and focused on my breath, my heartbeat, how far we had floated, the direction of the house. Behind us, a branch cracked in the wood. We both turned. Something scampered into the undergrowth—a rabbit or deer, probably. I continued to scan the trees behind us. After a moment, he spoke again.

I'll pee on it if you want.

I snatched my arm from his grip. —Oh scram. I've had enough of your ideas.

Jellyfish tentacles have thousands of sting cells called nematocysts. To deactivate them on the skin it's best to apply vinegar. Urine's second best.

This is your fault. Let's go back.

How long will that take?

I sighed. My irritation with him was increasing the pain. A string of bumps had flushed up my forearm. A sob welled in my throat. I bent over and let the warm tears spill on my wrist to soothe the burn.

Why don't *you* pee on it, then? he said.

It won't work.

It's better than nothing. I won't look.

He rotated on the rock and squatted in the opposite direction, out to sea. I realized I did have to pee, that I hadn't gone since that morning. I sniffed and wiped my eyes with my good wrist. Patrick whistled. A pretty tune I couldn't place, maybe a hymn. It comforted me—our silence, his whistling, the waves turning below. The sting hurt, but no more than the time I disturbed a wasp nest and got nipped three times on the thigh. Patrick continued to survey the sea. I fingered the button on my pedal pushers, then pressed it through the hole and pulled my pants around my knees. I pushed my underwear out of the way and released a stream of urine onto my forearm. It burned more, but that felt okay—like it sealed the sharper, isolated burns. A hot trickle dropped down the rock toward Patrick. I could tell we were both listening. Finally, I pulled up my pants. The damp spread in the crotch of my underwear, beads of it smearing onto my thighs. I felt proud. As if I had passed his test.

I think we're that way. He pointed left, where the bluff receded into dark needling trees.

He did not congratulate me as we walked, or acknowledge how brave I was. He stopped whistling and hiked a few paces ahead on the rock.

The urine had dried on my wrist by the time we returned to the house, releasing a light musk. The row between Mom and Eugene had subsided. Eugene had changed into swim trunks so he could wash the car. His stomach pouched over the waistband, black hairs crawling from his belly button, the sun lancing off his shoulders. Mom dozed in her striped deck chair with a lime soda on the table beside her, a book folded over her ribs like armour. Joan and Kenneth lazed on the grass with a pineapple, Kenneth prying reedy wedges with his Swiss Army knife, passing them to Joan, who sucked the fruit and whipped the husks at the Gravenstein. Patrick hadn't said a word on the walk home. Now he knelt on the grass and prodded the hydrangea bush. Something filled his hand. I recognized it then—a fragment of the dollhouse roof.

Where'd you find that? I asked, too loud.

He shushed me.

You wrecked it, I said.

He shoved me inside, past Luke and his rock tumbler. My brother pretended not to notice. He lay on his stomach before two piles of stones, one raw from the beach, the other glossy as marbles. I sprinted up the stairs—shaken by the sight of the dollhouse, overwhelmed by this insult to my dad, even if he never knew it.

Hardly a second after I stepped into my bedroom, Patrick slammed the door and shoved a chair under the knob. —You won't say a word, he said. About the jellyfish either.

I barely heard him; I was thinking about how Dad had spent hours sanding the wood and fitting the walls together. He even cut drapes from the fabric Mom had used for the real curtains.

Patrick leafed through my dirty clothes on the floor. After a moment, he shoved a long-sleeved shirt in my hands. Then I saw what he saw—a manacle of stings had branded my wrist. Slowly, widening the sleeve so it wouldn't chafe, I pulled the shirt over my head.

How do I know you won't tell? he said.

He sat in silence a few moments, the itchy blue of his eyes settling on his lap as he turned the roof fragment in his hand, the skin between his thumb and index finger moist and catching light, blistered from the paddle. He motioned for me to sit beside him on the bed. I joined him there, my heels tucked under my bum. He took my hand on his knee and turned it so my palm faced the ceiling. Then he pressed the broken wood into my skin.

What are you doing? I yanked my hand away.

He snatched it back, pinning my wrist on the bed, then grabbed my other arm, the one with the burns. The pain made me gasp. He closed my fist around the splintered pine and together, with his force, we pushed the point into my hand.

I closed my eyes and waited for the skin to break, but he released his grip.

I'll give you a choice, he said.

Outside the room, dishes clattered for lunch, the kettle boiling, Joan arguing with Mom in a shrill voice, Luke trying to show both of them his stones.

You will have to do something so embarrassing you

would be ashamed to tell, he continued. But don't worry. You do it every day.

What?

Relieve yourself.

Are you bonkers? I already—

Not that way.

We fell quiet. I waited for him to crack a smile and say, Got you, but his expression remained fixed.

You can clean off in the bathroom after.

I snatched the wood from the bed and dug it into the heart of my palm. The edge was dull. I could feel a divot where the skin had bruised. After thirty seconds, I couldn't press any deeper. I released my grip and hucked the piece under the dresser.

Patrick smiled kindly. —I'll give you privacy, he said.

The door clicked behind him. I sat on the mattress and stared at the wall, the crocheted sparrow and pine cones, the painting of a young girl kneeling before a tide pool, and thought: Okay. I can do this one thing. Soon it would be over. I detected movement in my guts. Often I can't go easily—not every day— but the adrenaline loosened the guck from my intestine and I could feel it shifting. I removed my pedal pushers and squatted on the carpet with my underwear still on and pushed. The vulgarity of the action made me want to laugh—it excited me in a strange way. I could pass all of his tests, even the naughty ones. With one more push, the feces slinked out of me and filled the crotch of my underwear. It felt hot and dense under my bum cheeks. I started to laugh. I clutched my panties under me so the poo wouldn't slip out and opened the door for the bathroom. Patrick stood there, facing me. He looked down at my hand, his nostrils flaring. He stepped out of my way and I ran to the toilet.

Before the brothers arrived, Joan, Luke and I built the beach
fort together. We found swoops in the trees to lounge in,
brought pitchers of lemonade so we could nestle in the
branches with cold glasses in our palms. We climbed on each
other like bodybuilders; we practised headstands, we watched
sailboats through binoculars, we counted bald eagles, we built
fires from moss and dry seagrass, we dug bait, we dangled
worms from our hooks, we caught crab in wood traps. They
were larger than our hands, but we turned them over to check
the underside triangle; we tossed the rounded triangles back
to the sea where they drifted to the sand on top of each other.
The summer we met the brothers, Luke started to shine rocks
by himself. He organized his stamps in a leather binder. Here
and there he followed us.

I was late for lunch because I had to wash in the basin and
bury my soiled underwear in the earth where no animal would
smell it. For lunch, Mom and Joan made devilled eggs and
ham sandwiches. I wasn't hungry. A bilgy sweetness clung to
my fingers, though I had soaped my hands.

When I sat down, Eugene was lecturing his sons on the
Senate race in California. Kenneth had stuffed an entire bread
roll in his mouth and gnawed at the dough with his jaw open.
Patrick ate his salad with a knife and fork—slitting each
cherry tomato in half, lining them up on a leaf of lettuce. At
the same time, he read from a book open on his lap. No one
seemed to think that was rude. I had seen the spine the night
before—a pocketbook of quotations. When he spoke to
adults, he sounded so articulate for an eleven-year-old; I wondered if he had woven entire quotes into his speech. Some
words sounded awkward on his tongue, as though he had
never heard them aloud before.

Patrick, are you listening?

Yes.

What did I say?

His eyes moistened, as if hurt by the accusation he was lying. Eugene stilled his eyes on his son, and within seconds, Patrick looked bored again. That's how I knew he was faking.

You were discussing the leading candidates, he said.

I'd never heard the word "candidate" before. It had a lovely sound—how the syllables lingered on *can* before falling. *Can*-di-det, I repeated to myself. I wanted to remember. *Can*-di-det.

I don't like either of them, he continued. No one else noticed how he read from the book. —They have all the virtues I dislike and none of the vices I admire.

Eugene's cheeks tightened. Kenneth rolled his eyes at my sister, who smiled receptively.

—Of course he's listening, Mom said. Good boy. Do you want a sip of my mimosa?

Luke chewed a devilled egg with his mouth open and washed it down with lemonade, crumbs of yolk and paprika sprinkling his lips. As if to break the silence, he said, Mom, is Willa not eating because she's poisoned from the jellyfish?

Patrick looked up sharply. I felt an urge to step between him and my brother. I stroked Luke's chubby elbow and said, Don't be silly.

I saw from the cliff. It was bigger than your head.

He pulled his arm away to indicate the size.

Eugene wiped his mouth and leaned on his elbow. My mother spoke before he could, refilling Luke's lemonade. —Don't tell tales, darling.

I'm not. Show them your owie.

Patrick's stare pressed into me now. —Luke, I said, trying to wring the panic from my voice.

They were in a boat and a jelly stung Willa's arm.

He reached for my hand on the table. I let him push up my sleeve. Joan gasped—the sores had spread and looked irritated, as if my entire arm had been wrung with barbed wire.

It looks worse than it is, I said.

Patrick made her, Luke said.

My brother climbed from his chair and shot outside. The table fell into a stiff silence before he returned with a fistful of leaves and wall fragments. —First he broke the house, he explained, as if the two events were causally linked.

Patrick eyed his plate with a sort of impatience. My mother reached for the shards in Luke's hands, rubbed a strip of pine with her thumb, Joan dabbing my arm, telling Kenneth to bring ice wrapped in a cloth, Kenneth reaching for another devilled egg, Eugene reddening from his chair, eyes bright with anger.

Get up, Eugene said. He marched Patrick by the elbow into the study—Eugene's footsteps stuttering from his bad toe. I followed. I watched from the open door as he clipped Patrick's cheek with the back of his hand.

Say "ah," he said.

Patrick opened his lips. His father lay a roll of pennies widthwise on his tongue. The paper wedged his cheeks apart. When he saw me in the doorway, it looked like he was grinning.

2

Salt Spring Island and San Diego, California

I DIDN'T SEE PATRICK AGAIN until three years later, when we drove to California for Kenneth's high school graduation. San Diego sounded exotic to us, though it echoed the Spanish of other islands like Quadra, Galiano, Cortes. The brothers had boasted of their beaches—you'd never cut your heel on a barnacle; wagons parked on the beach to sell ice cream; women had hair the colour of white sand; men were so strong they carried women on their shoulders; children learned to surf before they learned their times tables.

In the week leading up to our trip, Joan and I lay in a circle of plum pits and cut moon-shaped faces from *Silver Screen*s she bought in Victoria. She thought she might get discovered in California; I promised to move with her. We would live in a sun-washed walk-up with plastic flamingos and palm trees, a vine of watermelon that drooped off the front porch. She told me about the stars while I ate wet segments of melon I'd packed from the kitchen—*This is Ava Gardner. You liked her* *in* The Killers, *remember? Her parents were poor tobacco farmers from North Carolina, isn't that stunning?* She had taken to the word "stunning" that summer. *Oh—Lana Turner! I love her, don't you? What a stunning black stole.* To me it looked as if a black cub had wilted around her collar. I shrugged and flicked a watermelon seed into an empty bottle of Mountain Dew. It made sense we should save them, I thought. So we could plant a patch when we moved.

Dad had pinned brochures for California on the walls of his old office in Victoria: a bodybuilder squatted on the sand and steadied a blond woman on his lap. She arched back with one hand on her hip, the other stretched above her, her feet pressing into his thighs. A second man stood on his hands upside down over her belly button. In another poster, a woman flew between two men, her arms opened behind her like swallow wings. Then a poster of Manhattan Beach, which wasn't anywhere near Manhattan: the road dipping to the pier like you could drive right into the sea. And all the blinking neon, the smooth Chryslers, women with gold thighs and muscular bums, men lifting dumbbells, cars parked on the sand.

The weekend before we left, our Sunday school teacher asked Joan to describe the three heavens. Joan recited from her notebook:

The first is the realm of birds and clouds that circles the earth. The second is the space beyond, where you'd find the sun, moon and stars. The third heaven, she said, is a thousand miles south of here on the I-5, where beach bums tan and surf and sing holy holy holy. Miss Edgar was not amused. She asked Joan to copy the correct description of heaven onto the blackboard and didn't notice that she changed the words: *it shone with the glory of famous people, and its brilliance was that of a precious jewel, like a jasper, clear as crystal . . . the nations will walk by its light and the kings of the earth will bring their splendour into it. On no day will its gates be shut, for there will be no night there.*

If California was our promised land, Patrick and Kenneth were prophets. Their figures gold and slender, their ears and eyebrows on an even plane, eyes glimmering blue like the sun on oiled nickels. Their clavicles ran the length of their shoulders. Pea-sized notches marked the centres of their bodies, their stomachs so lean you could see the divisions of their abdomens. Their shoulder blades were wing bones. I expected their arms to start pounding and lift them up.

It took three days to drive, sleeping in motels with bony mattresses, eating pancakes at roadside cafés, buying baskets of blueberries from farm stalls, our fingers blackening with every handful as the fruit decomposed in the heat.

Kenneth's graduation ceremony was long and hot. We circulated the same metal flask of water, dabbing our foreheads, fanning our chests with the paper programs until they finished calling students across the stage. Eugene's ex-wife appeared, and Mom excused herself to the restroom. Joan greeted her—a blonde who used to model for Colgate toothpaste. When I waved to Patrick, he didn't respond. I went over to him and said, Hi. How's it going. He stared through me as if he could see to the other side of my skull and said, Back later, Mom. I'm going to catch up with Vincent.

The next day, Eugene took all of us to the zoo. The boys arrived in a pack of high school friends, whose tickets Eugene was forced to buy. Again, Patrick pretended not to hear when I called his name. They all stared at Joan. I remember she wore tapered slacks, Mom's eggshell blouse with the scalloped collar.

Her cheeks had turned already, as leaves turn. The sun collected on her shoulders—a dust down her back that pinched each nut of her spine. I have come to recognize this week in California as the fulcrum, this moment at its centre, beginning to tip. On one side, Joan and I bathed together, dipped in the cold lagoon, spread our bodies over the grass like tablecloths. On the other side, Joan stood in our mother's clothes. Her hand pushed the curl that kept falling back into the crown of her new sun hat. She ignored me when I said the brim looked like a flying saucer, when I hummed the theremin tone from *The Day the Earth Stood Still*. She turned fifteen that summer, but we shared eelish hips and swimsuits. Under Mom's blouse, Joan's spine was a column of limpet shells.

Luke bought popcorn and peanuts in a cone. He ate like the chimp ate, his mouth banana'd so he caught every nut. When he chewed this way at home, Eugene stared at Joan until she told Luke to stop. I couldn't see Eugene in the concession line, where he'd gone to buy Mom a Sprite. Mom had wandered down the path to the bear cage. She stood nearer to the cage than the other mothers. The other mothers juggled lemonades in their fists, fried dough, a stuffed penguin, their child's palm. Mom leaned with her back against the fence, her fingers fidgeting to loosen her collar. When she freed enough skin, she fanned a copy of *Zoonooz* against her throat. The bears posed behind her. One sat on his tailbone and clasped his heels. Another swayed on his hind legs, front paws shined out. His stance mirrored my mother's, who turned to grip the fence with both hands. A third bear pressed his paws together in prayer or clapping. They moved only as much as they needed not to fall.

On the central boulevard, a peacock weaved through the crowd. At first no one but me saw him. He wound between bare shins and espadrilles, a woman's sandals. I worried a heel would puncture his neck. Only Joan followed my gaze. His thousand eyes swept aside corn cobs and drink straws, the oily papers from doughnuts. A lollipop stuck to his tail. Joan scooped a handful of popcorn from Luke's cone and bent to feed the peacock. The bird stabbed his beak into her palm. Later I saw the holes he made, as if he had filled her hand with seeds.

Eugene found Mom at the bear cage. She clasped the bottle of Sprite to her temple. The peacock threaded between my sister's ankles. He sidestepped a child with a pretzel and picked his path toward the ladies' toilets. I wanted to follow him. Not to the toilets. I wanted to nap in the green hammock of his tail feathers. Instead, I went to find the Antarctic exhibition.

They had painted the pavement to simulate ice. There might have been real ice too, but I felt warm. The sun filled my eyes, and when I closed them, a locust shape drifted across my eyelids. It felt nice to be alone. Other girls my age, twelve or younger, stood with their parents and pleaded with them to buy bottles of Coke. Eugene'd given me a roll of pennies to spend. I could buy ten bottles of Coke. I stood in the centre of the walkway and watched the penguins. They spat back and forth on their water chute.

After the Antarctic exhibit, I found the others still waiting at the bear cage. My family stood away from the other families, collected as if by accident. No one spoke or shared a point of focus. Only Eugene watched the bears. My mother tipped against the cage, her eyes closed, the bottle of Sprite dangling from her fingers. Luke crouched on the dirt and lured a woodbug up his arm with a corn kernel. Joan stood apart from them and searched for me, or the peacock, which had disappeared in the same direction. Kenneth and Patrick bummed on the table outside the concession stand with their high school friends. Energy hummed through them, pushed the boys to jostle and wing onion rings in the air. The boys, too, looked like locusts. A nicotine swarm of jeans, hair parted at the back. In time, Joan would call this a ducktail. She would oil Kenneth's hair for him, comb it into quiffs. He watched her now. Cigarettes passed between the boys' fingers. Patrick tapped his ash into a Coke bottle, then in the part of another boy's tail. Unlike my family, the guys shared a point of focus. My sister did not realize her braid sagged from her hat, the end still tucked so the hair looped down and up in a sling. This one imperfection undermined how carefully she stood, her breast lifted, the heel of her front foot nestled in the arch of the rear. It made her look vulnerable. But she knew she was watched. Their gaze lifted her into a new dimension. She found herself in their want: an ideal cast of herself. Their want changed her. She saw her body in gold and spun toward this image.

That evening I watched her dress. I asked her, When the sun's bright, do you ever see a locust inside your eye? She said, Willa, there's no such thing as one locust. Locusts are swarms. She missed the point. What if he belonged to a swarm? What if he fell behind? But she was no longer listening. One locust is a grasshopper, she said. She had traded her slacks for white beach shorts, Mom's blouse for an ice-cream-blue Orlon sweater. Mom scanned Joan's legs in the hotel lobby. It was too late in the day to display her thighs, but she didn't say anything. At Peking Café, no one wanted to eat. Patrick and Kenneth had plans for a movie, and Eugene wouldn't let Joan go. In protest, she hardly spoke. Even Luke sat quietly. In

each well of silence, Eugene ordered another dish. Orange
chicken, tomatoes and beef. The plates began to crowd our
table. Pork chow-mein, he ordered. Spring rolls. All I wanted
was a bowl of egg flower soup, because I never knew eggs
bloomed flowers. I wondered if they looked like daisies. I
played a game where I ate the rice off my plate grain by grain.
Joan parted the noodles with her fork and pushed them to
the side of her plate.

Willa, said Eugene.

I looked up in surprise.

How did you like the bears?

Pardon me?

Which bear did you prefer?

Eugene did not typically pose questions to me. He preferred to ask Mom or Joan.

I'm not sure.

I liked the tall ones, he said.

No one replied. I wondered if he meant the bears on
hind legs.

Joan sliced a flower of broccoli and flattened the buds
with her knife. It looked like a peacock fan. One thousand
eyes, so green they were nearly puce. As our silence thickened,
Eugene waved down the waiter, who wore a pale waistcoat.
I expected to find the fabric marbled with sauces and steams,
but over the evening, his vest stayed as white as his teeth.

Could we try an order of Mongolian beef? asked Eugene.

We hadn't eaten enough from any plate for the waiter to
clear space. Mom looked embarrassed. She had tied a pretty
scarf around her neck, but one of the knots was undone. The
corner of her scarf trailed her plate.

I leaned across the table and grabbed her scarf before it
touched the orange chicken.

She lifted her head.

Willa, don't reach, said Eugene.

I sulked back in my chair.

I thought they looked tired, said Mom.

All of us looked at her. Mom inspected the corner of her scarf. She pulled a loose thread, which tugged longer. She frowned and released the scarf back to her breast.

After a few minutes, the waiter returned with a plate of glistening beef. To make room, we balanced our dumpling saucers on the rims of larger plates. We balanced our teacups on the rims of the saucers. I could not see the tablecloth. I saw treacle marinades and bright lumps of pork.

I liked the elephant, said Luke.

Joan dangled a knife over her plate. —Because he had a long knob? she said.

Luke opened his mouth. He knew enough to be offended, though he didn't grasp why.

What? asked Eugene.

Joan stabbed a water chestnut with her knife and smiled at me as she chewed it.

What did she say? Eugene asked Mom.

But Mom was lost in her satellite of thought. The loose thread had latched to the chicken glaze.

Waiter, said Eugene. Could we have another plate of egg foo yung?

After dinner, Joan and I sat on the hotel bed with a bag of pears from the fruit market. I had questions for her, like would she marry Kenneth? What did she write to him on Mom's blue stationery? Did she remember when our neighbour Ko-Ko taught us to fold the paper into frogs? But I didn't trust who would answer. She sat like she always sat, her knees open, legs splayed on the mattress. Her hair held the same crimps as if pressed inside seashells. Yet I sensed she was not the same girl who dug clam gardens with me. We sat together like normal, but I did not know what words to say. An eyelash had fallen onto her cheek. I felt I could lick my finger, press the pad to her skin and remove the eyelash, and that action would come more naturally than speech. We could sit spine to spine and align our backs and fill the notches of each other's vertebrae. Our bodies had matured together like trees. Two trees shovelled into the same soil, competing for sun, limbs warped and forking, needles interlocked. This trip to San Diego instilled new hopes in her— new pleasures and vanities—yet our limbs wound the same loops, the same paths around each other's elbows.

What? she said, her eyes moist. From emotion or allergies, I couldn't tell. —You're staring. She lowered her gaze to the pears in her lap.

I leaned forward and wiped the eyelash from her cheek. I blew it off my finger and made a wish: to catch up with her. The thin spike drifted to the pillowcase. She passed me a fruit. Around us, the bedsheets matched the paint on the walls, green as the underside of a leaf, or bathwater. We knelt in the bathwater and smelled the bellies of the pears before we bit them. They were overripe, the skin bruised and gold. The fruit weighed in our palms like heavy bells.

That night, I lay under the sheets and she slept beside me over them. Her legs stretched long across the bed, a lavender brown like her arms. I woke to a pebble on the window glass. Beside me, the weight shifted on the mattress. I opened my eyes as she yawned and swayed her legs to the floor.

What are you doing? I whispered.

She raised a finger to her lips. —Go back to sleep.

I folded my arms across my chest.

She lifted her shorts from the floor and tugged them over her hips. I wanted to ask her not to go.

Shh, she whispered again, as if I did ask. —You're sleeping.

She kissed her palm to my nose and stepped outside. I watched the forecourt from our window. A boy stood beneath the tree in a blue baseball cap—Kenneth, I assumed. Her figure appeared. The moon paled her legs as she tipped up on her toes to kiss him. I could follow the line of her calves down the street long after his shape sunk into shadow.

The next day, we visited Eugene's yacht at the marina. I thought we might go for a sail, but he only let us sit on the deck and eat sandwiches. He stalked the length of the schooner, his bad foot dragging a second behind the other one. He slapped the masts, thick as tree trunks, tugged at odd ropes. I began to suspect he didn't know how to sail, and exchanged a look with Joan.

Genie, she said, mimicking Mom's voice. —You ever take it out of the mooring?

Mom slapped her. Not hard, but Joan bit the inside of her cheek.

What's that? Eugene called from the bow, marching back to us proudly.

My sister dabbed her cheek with her finger, scowled at the deck.

She asked about the boat's history, said Mom.

He punctuated the floorboards with his loafer. —She was built forty years ago. For a treasure-hunting expedition to Central America.

Cool, said Luke.

He's lying, said Joan.

Mom raised her eyebrows at her, as if to say, You want another one?

There were lots of expeditions back then, sport. The Spanish kept their doubloons somewhere.

What's a doubloon?

A gold coin. Worth two escudos.

So did you hunt treasure, Uncle Eugene?

'Fraid not, champ. I bought her off a fisherman.

Why?

Mom pulled Luke onto her lap to hush him and said, Who wants a ham sandwich and who wants cheese?

Cheese, said Luke.

Ham, said Eugene.

I'm not eating, said Joan.

Me neither, I said, in imitation, adding a sigh to announce my boredom. *Greta* wasn't huge compared to the ferries from Vancouver Island. What was the big deal?

On the final day of our trip, Patrick and Kenneth arrived to swim at the hotel, though their mother had a pool at the house in La Jolla, the shape of a kidney bean. Kenneth wanted to see my sister and Eugene would not let her visit La Jolla without a chaperone. Joan had bought a new swim costume in town—white, ruched up the waist, strapless. I was stuck in my pilled yellow suit with a flamingo on the belly. I swam by myself in the deep end and practised diving for coins, which I dropped to the bottom before I dove from the deck, my eyes open under water. I could see their feet kicking from the other end of the pool, the suds from their heels and long calves,

Kenneth and Joan pedalling to tread water, Patrick floating a circle around them until he left to swim lengths. I resented them for excluding me, but I was a strong diver. I could enter the water cleanly and arrow to the bottom for the coin. Off the high board, I could even do a somersault. That was enough payback for now. I cut the air like a pelican while the others flapped below, muscling sloppy lengths. The hotel had plastered the bottom of the pool with a prickly material, which glittered sage from the surface. The four of us had the pool to ourselves, though a small girl played on the deck with a yo-yo while her mother blew air into an inflatable turtle.

Eugene had given us each money for a sandwich, so when my stomach started to growl, I climbed from the pool and padded to the change room. The café in the lobby sold apple pie and something called a Hollywood salad; I couldn't wait to sit on the terrace in my cat's-eye sunglasses and eat Hollywood salad like Lana Turner. I stepped onto the melon-pink tiles and rotated the shower tap. I had not brought my own soap, and the fluid in the canisters smelled of laundry starch. I pushed the straps of my swimsuit down my shoulders to rinse off, the water releasing from the metal head in hot bursts. That's when he came in. I thought he had walked in the wrong change room by accident—his orange-and-black argyle swim briefs that cut just under his navel, his chest still expanding with breath from the swim. At the sight of him, I gasped and clamped my arm over my breasts. His eyes worked across my arm to where I could feel air on the bump of my left breast, which my wrist wasn't wide enough to cover. A smile spread across his face.

What are you doing? I asked.

The spray fell like snakes from a barrel of water, down the back of my head and spine, and in a moment of shock at the sensation, I stepped from the shower stream. I had moved, accidentally, toward him, my hair slicking the side of my neck, my bathing suit slung around my waist, my breasts small yet so far apart and slippery I could not hide them. Carefully, Patrick folded down the waistband of his briefs and withdrew his penis, which was an even tan colour, like his stomach. In a graceful motion, he stroked the underside of his testicles, then tightened his grip around the shaft. He beat his hand back and forth, his face crimping into a terrible sneer as his eyes traced my breasts and waist, the pubescent fat below my navel, my thighs shivering together, the bottom of my swim-suit creeping up my butt cheek with every tremble. The display disgusted me, I wanted to sock him in the chin, run from the shower soaking wet, but I couldn't move, and as I stood there watching, I felt complicit. A warmth unravelled in my groin. He slammed his palm on the wall beside him for support and shook his fist up and down his penis. The way it had hung before stiffening reminded me of a toy elephant's trunk. This image doused the tingling sensation between my legs, and at the same moment, he groaned and released a sudsy squirt up his chest, a hot dime of it landing on my thigh. He continued to moan and rock his hand up and down as he buckled in half, breathing, and I snatched my towel from the hook and bolted from the change room.

3

1953
—

Salt Spring Island, British Columbia

ON THE FIRST DAY BACK, Luke received the packet of stamps he had ordered from a catalogue. He spent the morning categorizing them by country, measuring their perforations, stroking their gums. He knelt in a pool of light in the dining room, his leather album beside him, a magnifying glass, the flannel of his pyjamas wound around his knees. In his palm, he fingered a copper-shelled beetle on a blue frame. Cuba 1950.

In the study, Eugene folded his socks. He owned a delicate selection—calf-length, dandelion green. He did not fold them how Dad folded them, the way he'd learned in the war. Eugene pressed the socks together to fold them in thirds, then opened the elastic and tucked the toes inside. The pairs formed neat parcels, which he arranged in a row in his suitcase. I wondered who'd taught him to fold socks so discreetly. Eugene did not fight in the war.

The kitchen smelled sunny with coffee. No one had cooked, but I could smell the fragrance of other mornings.

Charred toast, sulphurous eggs, newsprint. Dad wiping yolk off his chin with a corner of the business page. I lifted the lid of the percolator. The basin was full—no one had touched it. So I poured myself a cup. The liquid smelled vinegary up close. I could not bring myself to sip, but I didn't want to waste the coffee either. I carried the mug outside.

Mom sat on the terrace swing in a network of afghans. The wool bound her feet at the bottom like a fish's tail. She drank what looked like cream from a whisky tumbler. A cigarette balanced between her fingers, Eugene's carton open beside her. She lowered her glass and smoked. After a studied drag, she tapped her ash into one half of an oyster shell.

Is that you, Will?

I stepped onto the terrace and shut the French doors behind me.

She said, Sometimes I think of you as a forest creature.

Like a metal, her voice warmed and cooled with her environment or whom she spoke to.

You know what I mean, don't you? she said.

I stared into the sunlight. She watched me blinking and smiled. I think I did know what she meant, but I didn't want to get it wrong. I let her continue.

I'm never alone in the forest, she said. Even if it's silent, I will find bushtits and minks and voles.

Bears, I said, thinking of the zoo.

Sure, bears. Mountain lions. Bryophytes.

I waited.

Moss, she said.

She smoothed her hair into place and sipped from her drink. She used to curl her hair and fold it inside a snood, or else plait a wreath behind her ears around the crown of her head. I was relieved when she cut it. I worried she would stop combing and her hair would grow stringy, and I'd have to listen to other women's comments at Ganges. Salt Spring Island was a small place.

You have to be particularly mindful of moss, she said.

She lifted the cigarette to her mouth and inhaled the smoke languidly. She had found a new kimono in California—honey pink, patterned with windows. Stained glass windows, grey windows, windows with birds. She released the smoke through her lips. The kimono's silk sleeves pooled around her elbows.

Have you brought me a drink? she asked.

Both our eyes lowered to the mug. I had nearly forgotten I was holding it.

Coffee, I said.

No, thanks, Ducky.

She lifted the mug from my hands and placed it on the table beside her. Joan and I used to play old maid at that table. It came from Grandmother's set of iron garden furniture.

Mom patted the cushion beside her. I climbed onto the porch swing. She lifted her glass, but paused before it reached her lips. She dipped it toward me.

Sip?

I took the tumbler with both hands, the ice bumping my teeth as I drank. The liquid tasted sweet and eggy. A curl of heat wiped my tongue.

Mom took her glass. She rocked it, watched the ice slide back and forth.

Now I'll have to get more, she said after a moment. She glanced at me, as if considering whether I could do it. After another moment, she combed my hair with her fingers and pushed it behind my ear.

Eugene's packing in the bedroom, I said.

She continued to rock the ice in her glass. The cubes plinked louder as they melted.

Big suitcase or little suitcase? she asked.

Little suitcase.

Okay, she said. Good girl.

But he's folded a lot of socks.

Has he now?

Yes.

Little suitcase, many socks, she said. What do we make of that?

She tried to sip from her glass, but there was only ice.

Maybe he wears two at once, I suggested.

She sucked a cube, then opened her mouth to spit it back. The ice was too wide to slip out subtly.

Willa, she said, after she had completed the manoeuvre. —Why don't you go for a walk?

She rested her head on the back of her wrist.

Pick us some flowers, she said as she slouched, her knees nudging me off the swing. The kimono had unfurled around her heart, and I couldn't help but pinch the collar together.

Your fingers are cold, she said.

I paused, my hand between the silk and the bars of her chest, her muscles tensed. I stepped back into the sun.

Dad had built the house on Salt Spring Island's North End. It was wide, with six French doors across and as many windows—you could see the ocean through every pane. Mom furnished the main room with her mother's antique chesterfield, the leather creased like an old face, rubbed so raw in patches the material had callused. It sat opposite a rocking chair my dad had constructed from driftwood and the set of

nesting tables where Mom had kept the dollhouse. The ceiling of the main room tented up like a wooden big top, painted
sesame, carved into triangular panels that seemed to billow
within the dome like the sails of a boat. Dad had seen the
style on a business trip to New Zealand, and he spent months
on the designs and construction—he would disappear to Salt
Spring for entire weeks while Joan and I attended school in
Victoria, the neighbour cared for Luke, and my mother pud-
dled on the sofa, occasionally rousing herself to snip peonies
from the garden, cramming the old, clammy bouquets in the
trash. Dad originally planned all of the rooms for a single
floor, but toward the end of construction, he decided to add
a second storey behind the main dome. This extension was
shoebox in shape, like the lifeless high-rises sprouting in
Vancouver, but Dad hid the hard edges with a thick arm of
wisteria and other vines sucking the wood. We each had our
own room at the beach house, Joan's the largest with a double
bed. I used to climb in with her so we could tell stories at
night or tickle each other's back. Luke had his own room with
sailboats painted on the walls, near the bathroom because he
had trouble reaching the toilet at night. Sometimes he
dragged his sheets to the tub, then lingered at our door until
I tented the blankets and he wriggled in beside me and our
bodies grew so warm, Joan kicked off the duvet.

Dad let us live like beach clams. We burrowed in the sand
and sucked nutrients from the salt, sand fleas exploring our
noses like luminous shrimp. We built clam gardens. We
cleared the rock from our beach and constructed a wall. The
clams stretched their tongues and spat water between our
toes. Joan told us they did not have tongues but feet. We saved
them from gulls so we could gather the shells ourselves in
a beach towel. Smooth, sombre clams, their shells ringed as

trees. I heard them ticking inside their cases. It felt hard to believe these were live creatures, not lockets you slung around your neck. My sister gathered them in the belly of her dress. I cupped the shells to my ear and waited for the foot to swab my cheek.

Until Dad left, he and Eugene worked together for the Puget Sound Navigation Company. Eugene lived in California at this time, but travelled to Seattle regularly for work, and bought a house there. Together, he and Dad negotiated the purchase of auto ferries from San Francisco Bay. That was in 1936, one year before Mom and Dad married. Dad moved out three years after the war. It wasn't until later I realized Eugene had already left his wife and moved to the house in Seattle full-time, that he had seen my mother while Dad was overseas. He hadn't fought in the war himself because of a bad foot from polio. When Dad left, Eugene took my mother for dinner once a month and joined us for a week at the beach house. I had thought it was out of charity.

Washington State bought the Black Ball Line in 1951, and Eugene moved to the Canadian subsidiary company, Black Ball Ferries. He ran the boats between Horseshoe Bay in Nanaimo and Gibsons Landing on the Sunshine Coast. Joan and I sailed the first crossing of the Quillayute three years after Dad left. I remember we wore Easter crinolines and white socks. Mother bought strips of chiffon to tie our hats down in the wind. In Gibsons, they had threaded the streets with bunting and provincial flags. We drove off the ferry in a parade of pipers and two brass bands. Spectators sang "God Save the Queen." Children jammed the sidewalks—boys in striped jackets and Sunday shoes, girls with their hair curled into perfect sausages. And I could smell sausages. Some of the ladies' groups had set up food stalls. The children watched as we passed. They did not wave because their palms were filled with wedges of yellow cake. They stared at us and licked their fingers. A Scottie dog capered after our car and barked. The pipers led the cars to Bal's Hall for the luncheon. We found fewer children there. Aside from a few infants in prams, we were the only ones. The waiters served watercress sandwiches and roast beef. Joan and I knelt under the table, flanked by twill trousers and nylon shins. We inspected their shoes. I could have sat there all lunch, but Joan felt silly, our legs too long. I remember two men boxed in a ring on the front lawn. We slipped outside to watch them before the waiters served lemon pie. The boxers wore copper shorts, their chests coiled with hair. One of the men cupped the other's jaw between his gloves. The other man grunted and locked his own bulbous fists around his opponent's neck. Their shoes stamped the mat; they orbited the ring. They looked angry. And also that they might kiss.

In a colander, I collected: honeysuckle, trilliums, a Nootka rose. Then I rested on my secret beach. Luke and I went straight to the beach house with Mom and Eugene after we returned from California. Joan stayed in Victoria for a week-long tap dance camp with her friend Linda, a poodle-haired windbag with skinny legs. They used to babysit me together. We'd sit in her polyester room and survey the Eaton's catalogue. Joan and Linda sprayed perfume on their wrists; Linda would lift her heels onto the bed and wipe the fragrance under her knees. She learned that in France, she said. The room always smelled like Chantilly and Cheez Whiz.

One of my goals that summer was to find a phantom orchid. Joan said only one hundred grew in the province. They bloomed in columns of waxy petals, no leaves. As if someone plucked the wings off a swan and wrung them into a garland. They preferred the soil you found under cathedrals of cedar. And compost piles, shell middens. I think it's the calcium. My secret beach had a shell midden. You could see it in the dirt that cut over the sand. Grass grew overtop now. Dad said the first people tossed their shells here after they ate. Now the shells had chipped into fragments small enough to scrape inside my fingernails. I liked to imagine who ate these clams. Ten thousand years ago, someone cradled this mollusc in her mouth and sucked a fringe of chewy meat.

Dad knew a lot about the island. He hired one or two guys from the village to help build our house, and they shared morsels of information, like the best end of the island to fish for salmon. There was a contract builder on Salt Spring, and it vexed him that Dad sourced the work elsewhere. City boy, he said. After cheap labour. But I knew Dad paid everyone the same wage. I proofread his books to practise my long addition. To be honest, I think he preferred the villagers' company. He knew the island's bays too, from his marine map, which Eugene had left pinned in his study. I memorized the map so I could find new beaches. My memory started to merge this map with his other posters. He would pin inserts from *National Geographic* and *Popular Science* on the walls—in case he needed to refer to a constellation chart, say, or a diagram of the human body. As I sat on the shell heap, I began to imagine the islands as an anatomy, a system of organs. On Salt Spring, we were locked in the centre. A pancreas. Vancouver Island loomed to the south and west like our fat, glandular liver. Across from here, Kuper was what? The gallbladder? Then Galiano to the east—our descending colon. Mayne, Prevost, Pender. I wasn't sure what those were. Farther south, Washington. The anus, I guess. On an island, it's easy to feel confined.

I couldn't see anything on Kuper from my secret beach. No houses or docks or pillars of smoke. It looked the same as any shoreline from here—a green feather landmass, edged with shells. Salt Spring appeared the same from the ferry, but up close this rock was a tangle of trees. The end we lived on, anyway. Dad cleared the wood at the front of our house, which faced the sea, but the rear was hemmed by firs and alders, boughs so thick they blocked the sun. On the beach, an arbutus grew sideways from the forest. I could walk across the trunk as though it were a balance beam. The bark peeled from the boughs like sheets of butcher paper. Some of those trunks grew so crooked with salt. They were my favourite. I liked the trees with trunks bent like spoons. I liked the forking trees. The corkscrew trees. Trees like a giant's pliant cutlery.

Dad left from the house in Victoria. He packed two suitcases and asked a colleague to collect the remainder. He sent a telegram from Seattle. I remember the messenger's trousers were cuffed in mud. Our lawn in Victoria did not absorb water well. I watched the boy kick the stand of his bike and step into a puddle. We rarely received telegrams to the house in those days. Even family sent mail to Dad's office. I remember the paper exactly—Western Union yellow. It smelled of envelope seals.

MORLEY WILL COME FOR REST

His last words to the family. I don't know what I expected.

Dad never said where he was going. I'd have gone to California if I was him. I used to visit his downtown office after school. He let me organize the brochures they collected from other ship companies. They always featured girls in the ads—women in swim costumes with bell-shaped bums. Women in rowboats, faces tipped to the sun, a woman in a nile green bikini, her arm raised, a starfish slipping from her hand. I filed the brochures by destination—country first, if applicable, then state or province, then each city. On Santa Monica Beach, the girls linked hands in the surf. They leapt into the air with beach balls. They waved from their towels on the sand. On the street, buildings were sun-bleached with frilled Spanish windows. Palm trees lined the boulevards. The ocean was everywhere.

It felt funny to dream about this from an island, where the ocean was already everywhere. But Luke and I were the only ones you'd see in the surf. It was too cold for adults, unless the day was very warm. The trick was to dive under and swim until you needed to come up for air. By that time, you would be used to the temperature, or deep enough that you needed to tread water, which helped. Sometimes the cold took my breath away. I tested my new vocabulary, which Joan taught me.

Fuck, I would say, my lips blowing out the consonants.

Sonofawhore.

Most vessels in the water were fishing crafts. They passed between the islands in dinghies and canoes, or larger boats, the floats of gill nets trailing in their wake like a string of tin cans. On the brochures for Canada, men stood in the sun and rolled up their sleeves.

From my secret beach, I thought I saw a canoe. Its bow rose from the water at a lean angle, like the throat of an ascending goose. It appeared unmanned. A bird shrieked behind me, and I turned to find seagulls jousting over a crab shell. By the time I looked back, the canoe was gone. The sun shone brightly away from the trees.

When I returned to the house for lunch, I found the terrace doors open. Mom and Eugene sat on opposite sides of the living room—Mom in the sunlight, on Dad's driftwood rocking chair, Eugene on the loveseat near the kitchen. I stayed outside on the porch swing to arrange my flowers. Sometimes I wanted to snip their stems and suspend them in a jar like carp. Then all the flowers would match the trilliums, which were ground blooms. I had picked too many of those. They wouldn't stand inside the vase.

They need you for a week? said Mom from inside.

I have a lot more to manage now.

Now?

Don't play dim, Dolly.

Dim Dolly, she repeated. What do they call that?

Who's they?

I don't know. Poets. Don't, dim, Dolly . . .

Are you drunk?

Drunk dim Dolly . . .

What's in your glass?

Drrram . . . buie, she said. Now that's a nice word.

I sat on the swing with one foot on the ground so I could push myself. I snipped the vines of honeysuckle with scissors from my sewing tin. It served as half sewing tin, half first aid kit: moustache scissors, two needles, a spool of thread, band-aids.

I don't even know if I should leave you alone with the kids.

Oh, Willa's very good.

I'm serious.

Then don't go.

There was a pause.

I invited the boys up.

We just saw them.

I know. But I spoke to Eveline last week. Pat's up to no good.

So?

I've asked him to man the house for a few days. Teach him some responsibility.

Why didn't you tell me?

I'm telling you now.

Who's looking after who, then? Couldn't hire a nanny so you ask your son to spy?

No one's spying on anyone.

No? What's he done, anyhow.

I strained to listen. Would he be coming this week? Had he already left San Diego?

Oh, you know. Public drinking. One incident with a dog. Are those my cigarettes?

Yes. What happened to the dog?

Didn't the doctor say to ease off?

Probably.

He continued in a low voice. I leaned nearer to the door.

Kenneth can't come. He's working at the marina.

I didn't hear her response—something brushed my knee. I opened my eyes. Luke stood beside me on the terrace, his arms folded around his stamp album.

Willa, I'm hungry, he said.

Hush, I'm eavesdropping.

Can you make me tomato soup?

Not now. Mom and Eugene are talking.

I patted the swing seat beside me and he climbed onto the cushion. He fingered the flowers in the colander, his hand tracing the five fragile petals of the rose.

Careful, I said. Watch the thorns.

Why didn't you tell me earlier? said Mom.

It's not your decision. They're my sons.

It's my house.

You mean *his* house.

In the silence that followed, I worried she would hurl her glass at him. Instead she said, Where are the matches?

Eugene didn't respond.

She sighed loudly and creaked off the sofa.

Don't waste those long ones on cigarettes, said Eugene.

Her match wiped the strip; I heard it from outside.

After a moment, Eugene said, Maybe I'll take Luke with me.

Beside me, Luke stared at his knees. He clutched the hem of his white-and-blue conductor shorts, the rose stranded across his lap. I draped my arm over his shoulder and pulled him close to me.

Mom still hadn't responded. Or if she had, I could not hear her.

Luke dipped his head onto my shoulder. I tried to hold his hand, but he gripped his shorts too tightly. I had to pry his fingers one by one. That's when I saw the wet strawberry of blood smeared into his shorts. He flipped his hand and opened his fist. We both stared into his palm—he had to hold it as a cup so the blood didn't spill.

I cuffed the back of his head. —You touched the stem, I said.

He nodded, eyes still fastened to the blood.

I told you to be careful.

The crease of his palm provided a shallow channel. I cupped my hands under his. Inside, I couldn't hear their voices anymore.

Come on, you ape.

We lurched off the swing like conjoined twins, my hands clasped around his palms as though we carried an egg. We hobbled inside through the kitchen doors to avoid Mom and Eugene, who still sat in the living room, though they were quiet now, their mouths wooden and still, bodies reclined on their doll's chairs. A drip spilled into my hand, perhaps because we were running, or trying to run, our shoulders twisted toward each other, away from our hips. We reached the bathroom and tipped Luke's hands into the sink. There was not as much blood as I thought. But his skin was hot with it. I ran warm water from the faucet and yanked a ribbon of toilet paper from the roll.

Hold this, I said. I crammed the wad into his palm. —Then I'll give you a band-aid.

I decided we should cycle into Ganges for ice cream because I didn't like tomato soup, and Eugene had opened a bottle of Cointreau, which meant they would smoke in stiff silence until they ran out of ice and Mom offered to walk to the neighbours'. Probably he would not leave today. Probably he would leave tomorrow, when his eyes ached and Mom refused to fry him eggs.

We bandaged Luke's cut and I wrapped his hand with a clean rag so he did not feel it on the handlebars. It was forty minutes to town—fifty with Luke, as his legs weren't long enough to pedal fast. I used Joan's bike, he used my old one. It was large for him—the wheels as tall as his hips. He looked like a cricket.

We rode down North End Road, between columns of trees that separated the road from farmland. Sun filled the leaves— the arbutus trunks plump with it, a warm gauze of light thickening the air between their boughs and the boughs of fir trees. There is a pigment where green becomes gold, I think. You see it in apples. And the gaps between branches. Between the branches, we saw brassy meadows and a pear orchard. The pears wouldn't ripen until August, but already I smelled the hard green of new fruit. We passed the schoolhouse, then the northeast lobe of St. Mary's Lake. Luke asked to go in. You could jump from the road, if you minded the nettles. I told him to wait until we bought ice cream.

My den chief said not to eat and swim.

I ignored him. I thought about how this island was the most beautiful in the world. More beautiful than California. Palm trees were unfriendly—their fronds like thin spears or paddle blades. I didn't like avocados much either. I'd rather eat a pear from the orchard, or a sweet, crisp apple.

What's your favourite ice cream? he asked.

I shrugged. The sun glanced off the lake and filled my eyes.

I like chocolate peppermint, he said.

I was not sure which I liked. I liked to say the words "burgundy cherry," and I liked how Mrs. Lee used whole cherries, which I tugged from the cream with my teeth.

Frozen custard with cherry, I said.

The sea smelled different at Ganges. The seagull shit and salt off the docks smelled pleasant, somehow. Organic like dead crabs. The scent mingled with vinegar from the chip shop, and waffle cones, boat bilge, the musk of warm ropes.

We ordered from the soda counter at the drugstore. I chose cherry. Luke asked for fudge. We stood outside the shop in the sunshine. The road was not gravel here, but warm and silty, like flour between our toes. We sat on the curb and tried to lick our ice cream faster than it melted over the lip of the cone. The boy who delivered for the creamery had parked his

wagon in the middle of the road. I recognized him. I think
he brought our milk last summer. As he heaved a can off the
cart, the sun lit the hairs that dusted his forearms. He didn't
look at me or Luke. Maybe we were too young for him to see.
He was older than Joan, I thought. Eighteen. His shirt striped
white and red like a boiled mint. His tan reminded me of the
brothers, but his skin tone looked more honest somehow,
from hefting crates and chopping wood rather than surfing.
When he bent to lift two more cans, the muscles in his forearms purled. I looked away as our eyes met. Blood flushed my
cheeks. I felt embarrassed by my bare feet.

Willa, said Luke.

What.

Your ice cream.

I looked to find it had melted down my wrist. A milky drip
of it, drying into a band of taut skin.

Can we go now? he asked. The boy had passed us into the
drugstore. Luke stood and petted his horse. The animal
huffed and several flies sneezed from his nose. I stood as well
and walked to the rear of the cart, where a blanket screened
the bottles from dust. I lifted a corner of the blanket.
Underneath, the boy had arranged the glass by size into rows:
tall bottles for milk and squatter vessels for cream that cinched
at the centre like hourglasses. I reached inside and freed a jar
of cream. I tucked it inside my shirt.

We cycled back toward the lake. I pushed the jar of cream
inside my waistband. If Luke saw the bulge, he didn't mention
it. We pedalled up the first hill, and I focused all energy into
my torso—into clenching my navel, as though my solidity
would stop the jar from falling. We tipped over the hill and

coasted down. I placed one hand over my stomach. The glass warmed against my skin.

Luke didn't ask to swim, though I knew he wanted to. I felt bad, because I'd said we would stop, but I wanted to go home. I wanted to hide this cream under my bed, then tiptoe along the trunk of my arbutus tree and think about the boy who drove the dairy cart. We lived so far up the island. I wondered if he still delivered our milk. For the first time, I felt glad that Joan wasn't there. They loved her so effortlessly, boys.

Luke's gaze hung on the lake, which glittered beyond the horsetails and spirals of blackberry. I nearly braked, but pretended I forgot my promise instead. The water glinted sharply—at that moment, it seemed a lake reflected more light than the sea. The ocean absorbed light, held the sun. A lake spat the sun at you.

It took an hour to reach home because I rode one-handed, cradling the jar of cream against my belly button. Luke didn't say anything as we arrived. He walked his bike to the garden shed and slotted it neatly beside the skiff. I slid my bike next to his. On his way out, he unwound the rag from his hand and folded it inside his pocket. Chocolate had dried into the corners of his mouth. He continued outside and crossed the grass, pausing on the porch to collect his stamp album. I followed him inside. Eugene had driven to the neighbours' for ice. Mom sat on the chair with an empty glass between her palms. Her lips were parted around a wedge of lemon.

4

THE MORNING AFTER Mom and Eugene made up, the kitchen: green stubbies like Japanese fish floats, Cointreau, a reedy bottle of cognac. Gorged lemons on the butcher block. Sprigs of mint. Eugene had pestled the mint into the block, its dye filling the knife cuts. The counters looked like the beach after one of their parties. Except no one drank Cointreau at beach parties, I didn't think. No one mooched over the logs with orange-lighted martinis, limp coils of rind over their glass. I noticed traces of food too, which surprised me. They often forgot their hunger when they drank, or they squeezed enough citrus fruit into glasses to fool their stomachs. But I saw a briny, pearl-sized caper in the sink, and in the fridge I found a chicken breast so thin they must have pummelled it with the pestle too. It sat under an oily relish of tomato and onion. No one had touched it. I wondered if Eugene cooked in the night, then passed out. They rarely prepared enough for leftovers.

I sensed Luke was gone before I came downstairs. His door was shut, and I couldn't hear him snore. I knew the sound of his sleep: the depth of his breath, the film of snot that flickered in his nose. His Buster Browns were gone from the front door, and I couldn't find his cowboy hat. He wore his cowboy hat every time he took the ferry. In the jetsam of the kitchen counter, I spotted toast crumbs, cereal milk, an empty glass clouded with pulp. Mom would be sleeping, but I decided to check on her. Her room was normally off limits. I slinked down the hall and turned the knob—held it with my palm, so the click would not wake her. I slipped inside and guided the knob's release.

My mother basked in the centre of her bed. Her limbs soaked the watery light from the window—Eugene had opened the curtain, I guessed, in an effort to wake her. Or neither of them had shut the curtain the night before. Light can make someone so beautiful and so ugly. I didn't know that then. I hadn't seen my reflection in harsh light—my eye sockets illuminated, oily forehead, backlit pores. And when I stared at my mother, I did not catch how the sun matted the creases under her eyes and warmed her hair into wisps of nutmeg, and smoothed her cheekbones, so she did not look too thin, but fashionable, and her arms were not liverish and stringy, but gold and tautly wound. The sun filled her with a warmth that was not her own, but no less inviting. I lay next to her and absorbed the heat from her limbs, the light from the window, and tried to slip into the same dozy dream.

After a time, my stomach croaked. I slipped back into the hall. I was hungry. Part of me wanted to get hungrier. To let my stomach open inside my gut, the membrane trembling into void space until I started to float. I borrowed my mother's canvas shoes from the front door and walked to the road.

It was Sunday, I remembered, when I saw the ladies in their church hats. Every week, Pamela Rice drove her husband's Plymouth to collect her friends on the North End. Their

husbands attended too, of course, but they took Mr. Tobin's
Cadillac. They had fun this way—girls and boys separated, as
in school. The church was in Ganges, and Pamela Rice could
walk. She offered to drive, I think, so she could show off her
town car. Custard yellow, glazed as a doughnut. She looked
coated in sugar herself. She wore a front-button dress with cap
sleeves, a beaded hat and round, white-framed sunglasses. They
had parked outside the Tobins' farm. Wanda O'Reilly picked
her path down the drive with Mr. Tobin's wife, Mariko. Not
many Japanese had returned to the island yet. Even then, I
could tell Mariko was different from those who did. She'd married an advertiser from Toronto, who drove that Cadillac. She
wore day suits and called herself Ko-Ko.

These were my mother's friends. Before Dad left, we
attended church with them. Now she slept in on Sundays. I
kept waiting for someone to notice and collect me or Luke.
No one did. Mom still invited the ladies for tea every week.
They sat on the terrace and talked about their husbands.

I stepped off the road to let the Plymouth pass. Wanda sat
in the back seat and fluttered her sherbet fingernails. They
had rolled down the roof. Her scarf whistled behind her in a
slash of pink.

I continued up the road to the path that led to my secret
beach. It was overgrown with blackberry, but I knew the
opening and could get through without scratches. There was
a way you could train your body to weave through under-
brush—to skip over nettles and dodge errant fistfuls of thorns.
I had spent most of my summers here, and every June my
memory of the paths returned like a mother tongue. The
brush may have thickened, a tree struck down, but I still knew
where to swipe my hips or duck a low branch. That's why the
sight in the tree alarmed me. It was in one of the cedars

rotting from the inside out. Joan and I hid here sometimes, the rusty mulch peeling into our hair. We couldn't fit now, of course. Maybe Luke could. I had passed the tree the day before on my way to the beach. Now, strung to the trunk by kitchen twine, its neck opened, the fur of its chest unlaced, a small animal hung in the gap. And below, in the trunk's cavernous gut, a rabbit's head.

It was a wild rabbit, lean from its fast heart and a lifetime of running. I felt surprised by the pigment of its lining. The fabric fell from its throat a beating red. It did not seem we could hide such colour under our skin, but I recognized it. I couldn't think where until I peered inside the opening. I had seen this red inside my sister. Once, she had turned the lights on after Mom said goodnight, then sat across from me on the mattress. She slipped her underwear to one ankle and unpeeled her knees. Her groin was hot with thrush. We didn't know the name for it then. Her vulva gaped like the beak of an infant bird. Joan saw me hold my breath. I didn't know what to say. She thumped her hips on the bed and jabbed her crotch with her fist.

I felt a similar helplessness now. Who would have killed the rabbit? If they hunted the rabbit for food, why did they leave it? I stepped back and glanced over my shoulder. I needed to see every angle at once. If someone in this forest beheaded rabbits for fun, I did not want to meet them. I ran through the salal toward the shore. A few yards from the bottom, my foot caught on the root of a tree or a rock, and I toppled onto my chest. I lay there a moment, my head inches from the beach stones, my knees and palms stinging. Then I heard something behind me—a sweeping through brush. Hair caught on bark. I don't know how, but I heard a girl's hair. I froze, my belly sunk in green tangles. An arm of salal had snapped and needled my hip. I felt too scared to turn and too scared to keep my back to them. I sat up all at once—a clumsy torquing movement that skinned my knees.

Luke? I said, though I knew he was in Victoria.

I examined each branch, as though if I stared hard enough, the trunk would bend to reveal who stood behind it. —This isn't funny come out right now.

I looked over my shoulder again. My arbutus tree stretched from the bank. I eased onto my palms and knees and stood. That's when I saw what tripped me. Slugged in the salal, moss and branches uprooted by its gunwales, lay a canoe. I turned again.

Hello?

Then I bolted. I worried my knees would buckle before I reached the road. I clambered onto the gravel and spun around to scan the woods. I could only see the path I had torn behind me, the moss and loose earth turned under my shoes.

I arrived home to find the dairy cart parked outside our house. The horse stood in the tree shadow and huffed pollen from his nose. My breath quickened. No one delivered milk on Sundays. I stepped onto the terrace and peeked through the windows. I couldn't see anyone in the living room, but a record revolved on the turntable. When I opened the door, a loamy voice hummed from the speaker. *There is a balm in Gilead.*

My mother stood in the kitchen with an ice tray. She had fastened the hair from her forehead with a plastic comb. Her kimono fell open around her waist. She wore a slip. —Hi, Duck, she said as she twisted the tray. She unbuckled two cubes from the plastic and carried them in her palm to the counter. —One or two? she asked.

None, a man's voice answered. The dairy boy stood behind me in the doorway, his hair folded over his forehead like a conch.

I looked to my mother. She stood at the other counter now with the ice cubes in her fist. A bead of water rolled down her forearm.

Darling, this is Roy.

She dropped both cubes into her glass and reached for me. Water seeped from her palm into the sleeve of my sundress. I waited until she lifted her hand, then rolled the damp sleeve up my shoulder.

He gave Patrick a lift from the ferry.

Patrick's here *now*?

He's staying for a few days while Eugene's away.

Why?

He's had a long journey. Why don't you bring him a glass of milk?

She opened the fridge, her kimono sash dragging under the heel. It hung by only one of the belt loops.

The dairy boy shifted his eyes to the counter, where a pulpy fistful of rind had been disgorged from the sink.

You should throw fruit peel in the trash, he said. I had to stick a coat hanger down there.

Yes, you've been a godsend this morning, said Mom. What with Eugene gone.

I felt embarrassed she hadn't cleaned—olive pits and used lemons still scattered the counters.

She withdrew a bottle of Campari from the icebox, forgetting the milk. She poured the liquid into two glasses and filled them with soda.

So where is he?

Outside. They arrived a couple hours ago while I was dead asleep. Eugene didn't tell me he would be here so early! She paused to shake her head, mouth smeared into a smile. —So Roy showed him around the island—didn't you? Then brought his suitcase back.

She passed the dairy boy his glass.

He raised it to me. —He wanted to go for a dip.

I imagined him swimming where he liked. Pissing in tide pools. No one asked me how *I* felt about him coming. Yet a dark sliver of me wanted to see him. I ignored that feeling, the ripple of excitement, and focused on the dairy boy, who had miraculously appeared in my kitchen. He was beautiful, like the brothers. His neck slender but hard as clay.

Can I try? I asked, reaching for Mom's glass.

You won't like it, she said, but slid her drink along the counter. To prove her wrong, I tipped the glass into my mouth and sipped long from it. The liquid prickled my throat, then rose again as bile. It tasted like dandelion. Even still, I wanted my own.

Mom reached for me and stroked my hair. —It's prettier than it tastes, she said.

I set the glass on the counter and tried to smack the flavour from my tongue.

The dairy boy watched my expression as he sipped his own drink. He wiped his mouth. My own hand lifted and copied him.

I'm planning a party, Mom said.

Why?

A summer party, she said, as if that explained it.

Without Eugene?

She smiled without showing her teeth. —Of course Eugene's invited. Have you seen Roy's horse?

He looked thirsty.

Roy glanced at me but didn't move.

Would you like a pail for water? I asked.

Why don't you do that for him, said Mom.

My feet stayed planted. —Can you make me a butter sandwich?

Willa, she said. Isn't that something you can fix yourself?

In my bedroom, I checked my mattress for the vessel of cream. It remained where I'd left it, wedged between two boards of the bed frame. I lifted the jar. The mattress snapped back. I sat on the bed and unscrewed the brass lid. The cream smelled of butterfat. I dipped my pinky, the liquid coating my nail. I licked it off and dipped deeper, until cream filled the space between my fingers. Then I submerged my entire hand. To pry it free, I had to close my fingers like a beak. Cream spattered the bedsheet, the lap of my sundress. I licked a drop from my palm. I opened my legs and rubbed cream into the strips of my thighs.

I wanted to return to the woods and examine the dead rabbit. I thought I might find a clue. Did they use a flat or serrated knife, for example. Could I learn clues from the wound, the fray of its skin? Maybe they left something behind. The spool of yarn. A matchstick. The print of their shoe. The dairy boy would protect me if he came along.

The skin of my palm had dried tacky. I padded downstairs to the lower washroom and rinsed my hands under the faucet. I could hear Mom's voice on the terrace and followed it down the hall. Dad's chair sat in the middle of the living room. I didn't like the look of the driftwood when no one sat in it— the brittle fingers of twigs and dead branches. It looked like a rib cage. A vacant torso. Mom and Roy perched on either side of the outside table, their thighs crossed and threadlike, glasses half-filled with pink soda. Mom leaned over the table and wiped the bow of Roy's chin. Didn't he go to church? I wondered then. Why was he free on Sunday anyhow?

Neither of them noticed me in the rocking chair. On the turntable, the needle had released and drifted back to the edge. I wondered if I should flip the record over. Outside, Roy drained the rest of his drink. He stood up and extended his hand. Mom stayed seated in her metal chair. She shaded her hand over her eyes, then reached her other hand to meet his. She rested her fingers limply on his palm, as though waiting for him to bow and kiss. He stepped away from her. Her hand hung in the air. He saluted two fingers to his temple and jogged down the steps to the garden. She swirled the rashy liquid in her glass and emptied it into her mouth.

She didn't see me as she stepped back inside. She tripped on a fold of the drape and swore. She stalked past my chair, rubbing sleep from her eye with the same hand that gripped her glass.

I waited until I heard her feet on the stairs, then I ran outside to cut off Roy. He had reached the horse by the time I found him. He was pouring a stream of water into the horse's jaw with a bucket from the well. The horse gnawed at it. His teeth mashed the air. Then he plunged his head and the water trilled down the channel of his nose.

Hey, I said.

Roy lifted the arm that held the bucket, startled. He looked at me under his bicep, then beyond me, as if he expected to find my mother in the window or watching from behind the trunk of a tree. Meanwhile, water coursed over the horse's eyelids. It wept down the seam of its jaw. When Roy realized his horse had stopped drinking, he jerked the pail back.

I wiped the horse's eyelashes and collected the moisture on my finger. The water beaded into a skin-coloured wart. I wanted to tell Roy about the rabbit, but I didn't know how to start.

Do you have anything to eat? I said.

He reached into his canvas bag and pulled out a tin of saltines. I took one and held it in my palm. I didn't actually want it.

You go to school? he said.

Sure. In Victoria.

He replaced the lid on his tin and tossed it back in the cart.

Do you want to see something? I said.

He was looking at me but not looking at me. —What is it?

I'll show you.

Is it far?

No. Just down the road.

He climbed into the cart. He sat for a moment, as if considering whether he should leave. Finally, he gestured to the milk can beside him. The passenger seat.

Do *you* go to school? I asked as I climbed aboard and shifted on the milk can to arrange my tailbone.

No.

He snapped the reins and we lurched down the drive toward the road. He sat with his legs open like a cowboy. I wondered if he was a cowboy. He didn't look like the milkmen in Victoria. They wore leather-billed hats and white coats.

Are you a cowboy?

No.

Do you know Roy Rogers?

Never owned a TV.

I listen to his show on the radio, I said.

We parked the wagon where I said, and I led the way along the path through wheels of salal toward the tree. Roy's boots thudded behind me—I wasn't used to hearing such loud footsteps. When Luke and I explored the woods, he glided over the ground lighter than I did. I had taught him how to run like deer—how to spring away from the earth rather than thump into it. Listening to Roy, I couldn't help but stop to survey his damage. He had trampled a fern. His boots kicked up moss.

Is it close? he asked, when he saw me pause.

Getting there, I said. A fern frond nodded into the dirt. I knelt to lift its spine.

He stared at me. I self-consciously stood again. I walked slower this time. I was beginning to question whether this was a good idea. Roy felt like an intruder now. Like Patrick. He didn't even know to avoid the moss. I could see the tree trunk ahead of us—the side with the bark still intact. I wondered briefly whether I should skirt it—pretend we had taken a wrong path somewhere. Apologize and suggest we head back. But my eyes had already started surveying the ground for clues. We had come so close.

It's there, I said.

I picked my way over the system of tree roots. Roy stamped after me. But when I reached the opening of the tree, the rabbit was gone. The kitchen twine hung from the bark like a bloodied yo-yo string. Not even the head remained.

I don't understand, I said.

Roy stepped behind me. I could feel his body heat.

There was a carcass on that string.

What?

A dead rabbit.

I waded through brush to where I had found the canoe. I stepped carefully down the hill, too distracted now to explain. It had been right there. I could see the canoe's imprint—the snapped arms of salal and dented moss.

What are you looking for? he said.

I scanned every direction, searching for dead wood, a corner of the keel. I knelt and roamed my hands over the broken branches. Then I felt something soft. Folded in a socket of salal brush was a flap of cotton. The branches had been bent into a nest. When I tugged the flap, it turned into a mud-stained, flaccid elephant, sewn from a tea towel. Beside the elephant, in the same pocket of leaves, someone had wedged a metal comb.

I tucked the animal back where I found it. Only a child would take such care—to fold her doll inside a wreath of leaves. Only a girl. Instead of returning the comb, I slipped it inside the length of my knee sock. I didn't want to question later whether this was a dream. In its place, I removed the plastic barrette from my hair. I inserted it in the branches between the elephant's arms. That seemed a fair trade, I thought. It was a yellow barrette. I had borrowed it from my sister.

Find something? said Roy.

No. What I saw is gone.

I brushed the burrs from my dress and stood up. Roy stretched his hand toward me. I let him help me over the thicket.

5

THE GAPS BETWEEN THE comb's teeth were plugged with film from somebody's scalp. I freed a smear with my thumb. A hair loosened with it—a black thread shorter than my own. It stretched to the end of my chin. I sat at the mirror and combed my hair until a metal tooth snapped. I hadn't brushed that morning. My waves congealed under the top layer into one mat. I'd always wanted my hair to be anemic blond or black as coffee. I liked extremes. I thought beauty might exist in superlatives. The tallest and longest. The whitest and blackest. The roundest. The softest. The most blue. In the books I read, plain girls described their hair as "mousy." I hoped my hair was not mousy. If a book described my hair, I'd like them to say wolf-like.

He appeared in the mirror first—leaning into my doorway, hand in the pocket of his jean shorts, feet bare. I noticed his shins were smoother than mine, though he was fourteen now. Boys at school had started to grow hair on their legs, under their arms. Above the collar of his shirt, his throat dipped into a nose-sized hollow.

I turned from the mirror and involuntarily glanced at his shorts. When I realized it, I darted my eyes away.

How long have you been skulking around? I said.

Arrived this morning.

Your hair's not wet.

So?

Roy said you went for a swim.

It dried.

We fell into a mutual silence. He waited for me to invite him in, and I waited for him to leave me alone. Downstairs, Mom opened and slammed drawers in the kitchen. The sounds echoed upstairs, spoons and forks rattling in their tray.

I don't have to play with you if I don't want to, I said.

He smirked. I regretted the word "play."

He stalked into my room and sat on my bed. His back crushed the pillows I had beat that morning. He lifted his hip to remove a paperback from his pocket and started to read.

What'd you do, anyhow? To get sent here.

He continued to read. He didn't look at me once. He read every word, or counted the seconds it would take to read every word. I watched him—first because I expected him to answer, then because I had been watching him so long, the moment had passed where I could ask him to leave or leave the room myself. After a hundred and seventy seconds, he shifted his backside on the bed, as if unable to get comfortable.

There's something wrong with your mattress.

What?

He bounced up and down, the frame creaking under his weight. —I feel something.

A sweat wicked my neck. How could he feel the jar, when I couldn't?

Just a bit lumpy. Stop it. You'll break my bed.

He smiled at me a moment, as if he knew I was lying. Then he snapped his book shut and swung his feet to the floor.

Forget it. I have to take a dump. He walked to the door, then turned, running his eyes down my waist to my pelvis.

My cheeks flushed and I pushed past him into the hall. He followed, closing the door behind him, but I didn't look back, I ran down the stairs, vibrating with frustration. I breathed in, pressed my eyelids closed. When my heart stopped pounding, I smoothed the lap of my dress. I walked into the kitchen with my fists clenched.

Mom bent over the counter, slicing a cucumber so thin the discs folded over the knife. She still wore her kimono, though she had applied lipstick. A hook of pink the colour of her Campari.

There you are, she said. She had traced blue pencil along the bottom ledge of her eyelashes. It made her irises purple.

I was starving. I still had Roy's saltine in my pocket. —What are you making?

A face mask.

Oh.

Would you like one?

I'm hungry.

She plugged the new Osterizer into the wall. She had ordered it from an appliance catalogue in Vancouver.

I found a loaf in the breadbox and lined two slices on a plate. —You want some? I asked, pushing Patrick out of my mind, returning my thoughts to the dairy boy.

I've eaten, she said. I scrambled myself an egg.

If my mother cooked for herself, she only scrambled one egg. In a fingernail of butter, with parsley from the garden. Dad used to nag her—*one* egg. Who scrambles *one* egg. I carved the crusts off my bread and left them on the butcher block, because I knew sometimes she liked to eat them when no one watched. She worked beside me, sliding her cucumber into the Osterizer, leaving six discs for me on the counter.

Thank you, I said. I spread cream cheese onto my bread. We still had a container of it from when Pamela Rice made icing for carrot cake. —Will you really throw a party?

Why not? she said. Wanda's thrown two parties in the last month. I missed both of them.

So?

She didn't answer me.

Does Roy go to church?

She spooned honey into the blender and used her finger to scrape it off the spoon. An amber balloon drooped off her nail.

I don't know, Duck. She licked her finger. —That's not your business.

Is it your business? I asked.

She bit down and scraped the nail between her teeth. —Don't be cheeky. She walked to the tap and rinsed her hands.

I arranged the cucumber petals into a flower.

She poured milk into the blender, sealed the lid and pressed start. The motor wailed. The blades sounded like they were grinding metal spoons. After a few pulses, she twisted the jar off the base. She pried off the lid and gave the wet pulp a slosh.

I made enough for two, she said. Sit outside with me. It won't keep.

I sliced my sandwich into fingers and followed her onto the terrace.

We sat on the canvas cushions of the porch swing. She turned me so that I faced her, my heels tucked under my thighs. She sat with one leg folded, the other stretched to the ground to catch the sun. I placed my plate on my lap.

Lean your head back, she said.

I couldn't help but wonder if Patrick was watching from some window. If he was listening to us. But I did as she said and shut my eyes. She spooned cucumber slush onto my cheeks, pushed back my hair, painted my forehead.

Willa, she said. She paused. —Charles slides down the banister and feels pleasure. If he climbs the stairs and slides again, does he sin?

I had no idea what she was talking about. The only Charles I knew was two grades younger than me and smelled of spinach.

Natalie rides her bicycle and feels pleasure, she said. She keeps riding. Does she sin?

My mouth felt dry. I tried to swallow but couldn't move the saliva with my neck hinged back. I think I knew what she was hinting at—and for the second time, I thought of Patrick. But it's not like Mom went to church. Isn't *that* a sin? Still, my cheeks warmed. I hoped the cucumber disguised it.

Maybe you should spend time with your sister this month.

I pushed her hand away and sat up.

Would you like that, Ducky? You could stay with her and Linda.

I hate Linda.

Don't be rude.

It's not rude. It's honest. I hate Patrick too.

She smiled and tipped my chin farther back. —Eventually, you'll learn when to be honest. She massaged cucumber under the bone of my jaw. —Your sister should be your role model.

I didn't understand. She told Eugene she wanted to keep me here, and now she wanted me to leave. My brow knotted as I worked this through, and the mask lumped.

She guided my head to rest against the swing. My stomach growled.

Cucumber really hydrates the skin, she said.

I closed my eyes and traced the edge of the sandwich bread with my finger. The swing creaked as her weight shifted. I opened my eye long enough to watch her massage the mask into her cheekbones.

See? She smiled at me. —Isn't this fun?

There were fewer mirrors at the beach house. That was something I always noticed. You became used to finding yourself on walls. The house on Salt Spring had belonged more to my dad, who furnished it with driftwood. Mom focused her energy in Victoria. Our velveteen parlour with pear-green chairs and man-eating drapes. She hung mirrors in every room. To make the most of the space, she would say. I liked them because they invited more bodies into the house. Our family doubled in size. Of course she decorated the beach cottage too. She brought the patio furniture and the striped sofa. But it would be trickier to pack panels of glass on the ferry. We had a mirror in the bathroom and one full-length in my mother's closet. But not in my room. So if I wanted to see myself, I had to lock the bathroom door and sit on the sink with my feet in the basin. It wasn't vanity as much as a game where I observed what parts of my body had changed. Eye colour, for instance. Today, could I see the ring of yellow around my pupils? How white were my teeth? Should I brush harder? Had the sunburn on my nose begun to peel? Of course I checked on other changes too. The hair under my arms. The flesh there. My breasts had spread in that direction—toward my armpits rather than each other. Not that I cared about cleavage. I didn't want to wear a bra.

Patrick's presence made me wonder where I stood in the family. People applied different words to Joan than they applied to me. They described her as a "heartbreaker." My mother's friends call me "sly."

I asked Joan what she thought once. She read a lot of magazines, and that made her an authority, I guess.

Say, what do you think of my looks, generally? I'd said.

She raised her eyes from her catalogue and answered so smoothly, I wondered if this was something she thought about. —You're owlish. Your eyes are too big, but I think you'll fill out.

Oh.

She leaned toward me, as if to kiss me on the cheek, then ruffled her hand through my bangs. —You're better off not thinking about it.

I had never asked my mother, but the next night she commented on it without my prompting. She and Joan had been at it. I don't remember why, now. It could've been anything. Every now and then Mom surfaced to say something sweet or mean to us. More often, she directed her comment to Joan, and more often, it was mean. She said things like, "I once saw a skirt *just like that*, on a whore in Vancouver." Or, "You'd be a lovely creature if only you fixed your teeth." Often Joan would retaliate. She'd say everyone knew Mom was a lush, she embarrassed the whole family, poor Eugene, what a banshee he'd ended up with. And Mom would tell her to get out, and Joan would go to Linda's.

So Joan had gone to Linda's. Eugene had taken the neighbour's dog for a walk with Luke. We sat alone in our kitchen in Victoria. It was dusk by then. Neither of us had closed the windows, as if to dispel the tension from their fight. The night smelled of the community pool and lawn clippings, as well as the cut lime and quinine from her drink.

Willa, she said as she wiped the sweat off her glass and

touched her temple. —It doesn't do you any favour to be beautiful yet.

I looked up from my notebook. I had been memorizing passé composé "to be" verbs.

The most beautiful women were ugly girls, she said.

What?

It goes to your head otherwise.

She squeezed the smile of lime into her tumbler.

Why are you telling me this?

You're a changeling. Consider yourself "bookish" for now.

Okay, I said, though I didn't understand what she meant by "changeling." I looked to her face for clues, but she appeared distracted by the lime, which she rotated in her hand.

You were always the better reader, she said. She tossed the lime over the counter into the kitchen sink. I started at the suddenness of the gesture. She wiped her palm on the table-cloth, as if to signal the end of our chat.

Since then, I sought myself in the mirror more often. What was the difference between me and Joan, anyhow? What made her beautiful and me bookish, or owlish, or sly? I thought I might try to be more sly. If I were not beautiful, I could be a changeling, as my mother said. I guessed it meant someone who shifted shapes. I had always admired the insects I mistook for leaves. I wanted to emulate them. I wanted to emulate the reptiles in hotter countries. The side-winding adder with scales like grains of sand. The pygmy seahorse, studded with coral tubercles. And chameleons, of course.

After Mom and I talked, I looked up "changeling" in my dad's Oxford dictionary. Here is what I found:

1. *One given to change; a fickle or inconstant person; a waverer, turncoat, renegade.*
2. *A person or thing (surreptitiously) put in exchange for another.*
3. *A child secretly substituted for another in infancy; esp. a child (usually stupid or ugly) supposed to have been left by fairies in exchange for one stolen.*

I liked that they put "surreptitiously" in brackets. Possibly I was a waverer, turncoat, renegade. The last one made me think. I thought back to this definition the morning after the face masks. That day was a day for being sly—for avoiding Patrick and finding whoever lived in the woods, to see if the barrette was still there. Maybe I would leave something new as a peace symbol. A jar of water, perhaps, in case they were thirsty. A sandwich—I could make a mean grilled cheese. I wondered how I could be *more* sly. I already stepped lightly. Perhaps I could wear more earth tones. I had a brown house-dress. It was a shapeless cotton thing—Joan said it looked like an onion sack. But today was not a day to be beautiful. I was a side-winding adder with scales like tree bark. A seahorse the colour of yellow cedar.

In the kitchen, I filled a mason jar with cold water and buttered two slices of sandwich bread. Patrick hadn't emerged from the guest bedroom yet, though it was eleven. I hoped to leave before he got up. My mother sat at the table in her kimono. She was smoking her morning cigarette and sipping coffee I knew had gone cold by then.

Lunch already? she said.

I heated a pan on the stove while I sliced the cheddar we kept in our fridge. I never saw anyone eat the cheese, but we always had a block on the butter shelf. Maybe Eugene ate it (surreptitiously) before supper.

I wouldn't make a habit of eating between meals, Mom said.

It was difficult to feel scared under such a pregnant sky. The sun warmed the top of my head like hot yolk. It made me think of that game we played at school, where someone cracks their fists over your head. *Dot dot, line line, spider crawling up your spine*, they say, running their fingers up your neck. *Tight squeeze, cool breeze*, blowing on your nape, *now you've got the shiveries*. That's when they crack the egg, and the yolk drips behind your ears. I thought about what Mom said about pleasure and sinning. I'd felt pleasure when they cracked the egg.

I located my cavernous tree trunk and worked my way back to where the canoe had been buried. I couldn't see it. Maybe the barrette had scared her off and she found another cove. After a few minutes, I found the elephant doll tangled in the same thicket of leaves. I unpeeled the leaves and searched the hollow between the elephant's legs, and below it in the scrub of branches. The barrette was gone. I looked around for other traces: trampled moss, grass broken back. I could see nothing. I left the jar of water and the grilled cheese, which I had folded in wax paper. The tide was out. I could walk to the end of my horizontal arbutus tree and jump to the rocks. The rocks opened into green sinks of tide pools. I liked to gaze into them and feed blackberries to the starfish. Today, I picked my way over the pools to the end of the point. This gave me a wide view of the sea between the islands, but the water glinted and I found it difficult to see. That's when the canoe glided past the rocks, its bow like the throat of a goose. A small girl knelt in the hull. She wore a cream dress, her hair clipped to her ears. Her cheek turned as the canoe drifted behind the rock. I caught a band of yellow in her hair—not a trick of light, I didn't think, but my sister's barrette pinning her bangs. The canoe slipped from sight. I wondered if I'd imagined the whole thing.

When I returned home, I saw another strange sight. Patrick was lying on the living room floor, and my mother stood on his back. She kneaded the ball of her foot into one of his shoulder blades, the hem of her kimono grazing the dimples behind her knees. Patrick's arms rested at right angles to his head, his chin and neck extended on the carpet. I froze in the doorway. He didn't wear a shirt, his back marbled from my mother's heels. She shifted her weight and raised her other foot. I expected her to keep lifting, Patrick in her talons like a limp trout.

I waited for them to see me. His face pressed into the rug; I couldn't see his expression. Had he complained of a backache? It wouldn't be the first time my mother boasted her talent for massage. She massaged guests at parties if she was drunk enough. But alone? With Patrick? Did he ask?

They'll bring wine, said my mother. All we need is one or two bottles of tequila.

She lowered her foot and paddled both heels into his sacrum. I missed the moment where I should have cleared my throat.

Patrick's eyes strayed across the room to the French doors. I followed his gaze, then found it mirrored back at me. I nearly gasped. He didn't say a word. Mother talked about canapés.

We'll get prosciutto, she said. We have a cantaloupe in the fruit bowl.

An energy passed between me and Patrick. At first, we only met in windows and pools of water.

6

OUTSIDE, THE HAND-DUG WELL. I leaned over the shaft and found black water, the bricks fleeced with algae. At the bottom of the basin, a finger of sun broke and turned. I did not see his face in the well. I saw it when I raised the bucket. In light, the water was clear and smelled of cedar. I saw my hand reflected first: the bones of my knuckle as I dipped my palm for a drink. I saw my mouth in the pail and the water that dripped off my chin. His reflection replaced mine as I straightened. I released the chain with a start and it dropped into the shaft. Patrick said he did not mean to scare me. I said he didn't. He said, Want to ask Roy if we can ride his horse?

Okay.

I can show you the wasp nest.

Okay.

He's not here yet. He's in Ganges.

Okay.

Is that all you say?

Yes. I mean no. I wondered if Roy felt pleasure when he rode a horse.

Later, the drugstore at Ganges. My face in the glass, pale as a sand dollar. The pharmacist wore a white coat. A woman stood at the counter. She had packed her motherly hips into a brown skirt that was tight for her. I could tell she was a kind woman. I could hug her without getting poked by her ribs. The pharmacist entered his room where he cut powders and pills. Behind the till, amber vials lined the shelf. The woman tried on sunglasses while she waited. No one stood at the soda counter. I could imagine the shop filled with girls like Joan, with yellow hair and side parts, or chubby-kneed children sucking malts through a straw. Roy had parked his wagon outside. He must have been in the back of the shop, delivering canisters of cream for Mrs. Lee. She made the ice cream herself—yellow barrels of butter pecan, which she wheeled out for church picnics. The pharmacist returned to the counter with a paper bag. The woman paid and walked out of the shop. I noticed she was still wearing the sunglasses. A voice asked if I had cycled all the way here. He stood behind me in the window. I hadn't heard him approach. His arms were tanned and did not reflect as brightly as my face.

Yes, I said.

Why didn't you tell me?

I don't know.

Roy's going back that way. He can give us a lift.

You already saw him?

We can throw your bike in the back.

After he gave us a ride, Mom made him an omelette. The kitchen smelled sweaty with burnt onions. Mom and Roy sat outside and slapped mosquitoes from each other's necks. I watched them through my mother's compact. Most of the powder had chipped away, but the mirror was a nice size. I could observe people while I fixed my face. Roy split the omelette with his fork and scooped a bite into his mouth. Mother chewed her mouthful and sat back. She patted her lip with her napkin. He did not notice that she had stopped eating. She touched his wrist. He looked up. She showed him how to hold his fork with the tines pointed down.

Patrick sat behind me on the driftwood rocking chair. —Are you watching him or her? he asked.

The next day, I wore shoes for the second time when I cycled to Ganges. One of Roy's canisters had spoiled, and he hadn't had enough cream to deliver to Mrs. Lee. He said he would have to deliver the rest of the load today. I left before Patrick came downstairs for breakfast. I wanted Roy to myself. I wore Mom's peep-toe sandals, my own blue pedal-pushers, one of Joan's wire bras. Her gingham top lifted past my midriff when I raised my arms.

The pharmacist stood behind the counter in his white coat. He bent over a newspaper with a stub of yellow pencil. I think he was filling in a crossword. No one stood at the soda counter. The shelves were crammed with sundae glasses, which mirrored the vials on the pharmacist's side. Between the two halves of the shop, I thought, there must be more glass than any other store on the island, except the pub. You could sit at the soda counter on stools or at one of three tin tables. A girl sat there now. I did not notice her at first. She had black hair to her chin. Thick eyebrows, which tented at the outside corners. Her cheeks were soft and long. She wore a striped dress. She sat by herself and ate a sundae from a tall petalled glass. Even through the window, I could see each topping: the beard of cream, chipped peanuts, a cherry. The spoon had a long handle. It bobbed from her hand like a cigarette holder. She looked up from her sundae and stared back at me. Her hair was fixed to her temple with a yellow barrette. Then Roy stepped from the back room behind the ice cream counter. He joined the girl at the table. I couldn't believe it. He bent over his elbows and watched the girl. She licked the cream off her long spoon. I hated her in that moment. Nibbling each peanut. Sucking the jellied cherry off its stone. He must have bought the sundae for her. I didn't know whether to leave or join them. She had already seen me, but he hadn't. She ate like my mother, carefully as a cat. The girl smiled. I walked in and sat in the last empty chair at their table. Roy looked at me in surprise. I avoided his eye contact. The skin around the girl's neck looked chafed. She loosened the collar of her dress.

Verne, this is Willa, said Roy.

Hi, Willa, said the girl.

Verne is staying with my parents.

Why? I asked.

Willa lives on the north end of the island. I know her mother, said Roy.

Verne lay her spoon across the glass.

I didn't know how long Verne had been there. She attended church with Roy's parents. No one spoke of her as gossip. Not even my mother.

The next morning, Mom sat outside in her kimono and sunglasses. I brought her a glass of orange juice, which she left on the table. Patrick had gone searching for a stick shaped like a Y for a slingshot. Eventually, I took the glass onto my knee and pretended I had brought it for myself. I sat beside her on the porch swing. Mom pried lint from her toenails with a metal file.

Where did the girl come from? I asked her.

What girl? she said. She examined the lint between her fingers and blew it off her thumb.

The one who lives with Roy's parents. Her name is Verne.

Have they tried talking to you?

No.

Do me a favour, Duck. If Roy's parents talk to you, scream the foulest word you know.

Okay.

What's the foulest word you know?

I thought of Joan's words. —Cunt?

My mother laughed. —That's a start. *Stay away, you witch-hunting cunts.* Say that.

Okay.

Now.

Stay away, you witch-hunting cunts.

Shout it. Pretend I'm Roy's parents. She pushed my shoulder. *STAY AWAY YOU WITCH-HUNTING CUNTS!*

So I introduced myself. I planned it for church the next Sunday, which Mom and Patrick never attended. I would sit beside Verne, and Roy's parents would invite me for lunch. I did not know how one would lead to the next, but I figured I would dress like a churchgoer and work the rest out from there. I wore pink. The dress sagged off my waist with an inch of extra fabric. I looked all elbows and knees, but I figured it helped if I appeared hungry. At the church, I leaned my bike against the fence and polished my Mary Janes on the grass. Soon, my mother's friends arrived in their Plymouth. Pamela Rice, Wanda and Ko-Ko. They wore suits the colour of pale vegetables, watery-cucumber blouses and skirts with buttons like corn kernels. I crouched back to my kickstand so they would not feel a need to say hi to me. They walked inside the gate, elbows linked, laughing brightly. I could not imagine my mother as one of them. Their husbands followed behind in the Cadillac. They wore banker suits. Eventually, I recognized Roy's parents. They were not so trim or rich as my mother's friends. They lived here all year round. Verne walked between them. Her eyes found mine right away. I fell into step behind them and followed them into a pew. My mother's friends sat nearer to the front of the church. They brayed to each other and tossed the hair out of their eyes.

We sang "How Great Thou Art" and "Holy, Holy, Holy." The pastor delivered a sermon about life in the garden. I thought he would talk about carrot seeds. It was a small island. We grew our own carrots. I thought he would lecture on virtues of self-sufficiency, but no. He meant *the* garden. "Then the eyes of both of them were opened, and they realized they were naked."

On the other side of Roy's parents, Verne was not listening. She sat with her knees pressed together and squeezed a mint wrapper in her fist. Her dress was okay—a light cotton with clumps of forget-me-nots—but she didn't wear socks or stockings. Like me, she only mouthed the words to the Lord's Prayer. I tried to catch her eye when we sat back down. She ignored me and stared out the stained glass window.

Roy's mother wore her hair in tight curls with bangs that barely filled her hairline. Her husband wore a loose brown suit. After the service, I turned to Roy's mother before she and her husband could stand.

That was nice, I said.

She looked surprised to be addressed by me.

I thought he was going to talk about gardening, I said.

She touched her husband's arm. —Harry, did you hear?

She thought the sermon was about gardening. What's your name? she asked.

Willa.

Willow?

Will-*a*. I'm here by myself.

Her smile fell, but she picked it up. —Are you hungry? We're going home for roast beef and gravy sandwiches.

I'm starved.

I stared at Verne, who pedalled her heel into her shoe.

Hi, I said. Is it Verne?

His parents' farmhouse was nearer to the lake than the sea. They had planted a stone garden out front with beds of fragrant needled plants like rosemary and edible thistles. A fence led around back where they kept chickens and six pigs. The front porch was lined with lavender. I leaned in to smell and nearly inhaled a bee. I held my chin there a moment, the sun on my eyelids, wings humming, the scent drowsy and full. When I opened my eyes, the others had already stepped inside the house, except Verne, who lingered on the mat and watched me.

They had two tables in their kitchen, a round table, where Verne and I sat with glasses of milk, and a long oak table with straw placemats. Roy's father hadn't come inside yet. He was in the coop counting chickens. They had been fighting, the woman said. Her name was Irene. The chickens pecked each other to death. She lifted a loaf tin from the oven with quilted mitts. Out the side window I saw Roy filling a metal basin of water for the dogs. They had three Labs, which I could smell inside on their nubby tweed couch. Verne flattened her mint wrapper on the table. The milk left a slug of white on her lip. Milk dried onto my own lip, and I didn't lick it off either.

I don't know why this felt like an interaction, like calling her bet in a game of cards.

Did you canoe here? I asked.

Her eyebrows sunk into a flat plane above her eyes. My eyes were darker than hers, I noticed. Her irises had an amber depth to them—resinous, like if I peered deep enough, I might find the wings of a moth.

No.

People often lied to me, and I pretended not to notice. But I wanted Verne to trust me. I thought she might also be sly.

Where did you find your yellow barrette?

Which barrette? she asked.

She wasn't wearing it today.

My sister's barrette. The yellow plastic one.

I waited for her eyebrow to lift, her earlobe to beat—the smallest muscle spasm to betray that I had affected her. But her face remained still.

Roy came into the kitchen. He kissed his mother on the cheek and leaned back against the stove. His eyes caught on mine—surprise registered on his face, but he didn't say anything. He turned to the icebox and poured himself a glass of milk. Irene gently pushed him away from the stove so she could drop eggs into a pot of boiling water. She passed him a plate of ruddy sliced beef and asked if he could lay the table. He carried the beef to the table with straw placemats. Verne stood and pulled a stack of plates from the cupboard. She dealt them on the mats, then circled the table again with the canister of knives and forks. I stood to help, though I didn't know where they kept their glasses. I caught my reflection in the window—the band of milk across my lip, Roy looking at me from behind. My cheeks burned and I wiped my mouth. Verne's lip was already clean.

At the counter, Irene sliced the bread, the steam unsealing

from the crust and winding into the air. I had never known anyone to bake their own bread before. Much less while they were at church. The dough smelled ambrosial. There was something about yeast and oven heat. I wanted to tear off a lobe and stuff it steaming into my jaw. Roy's dad hulked in from outside and washed his hands at the sink. He sat at the rectangular table and gestured for me to join him. I hesitated. If I sat opposite him, that would leave two chairs on either side—one on the corner and one adjacent—which left a fifty percent chance Roy would sit beside me. Alternatively, I could go to the bathroom and sit down on my return, but then Roy, Irene and Verne might have sat down already. So I sat opposite Harry. Irene set the bread on the table, along with a white Pyrex gravy boat. Verne sat at the end, between me and Harry. Roy sat on the other side of me. Irene drained the eggs and piled them onto a plate, where they clinked and rolled. I didn't look at Roy, but I could feel his warmth when I lifted my hand for a slice of bread. He smelled like sun and copper. I wondered how I smelled.

Verne, said Irene. Would you say grace?

I looked up to find Verne staring at my crab fingers pinching the bread too soon. I looked at Roy and he smiled.

Bless this food to our use, and us to your service, said Verne in a clear-water voice I could not help but listen to. —Fill our hearts with grateful praise. Amen.

It was the most I had heard her say.

The others murmured Amen.

Roy passed me the beef and our elbows knocked.

Pardon me, I whispered, though I didn't look up to see if he heard.

I listened to the president's commencement address on the radio, said Harry.

Irene leaned across the table for the salt shaker.

At Dartmouth College. Anyone catch it?

Our eyes travelled to each other expectantly, then rested on Harry. No one answered.

He was speaking to boys your age, Roy. You would have found it stirring. *Don't join the book burners*, he said. How do you like that?

Irene cracked an egg on the table and peeled it. She cut it lengthwise and sprinkled salt on the yolk. —Do you think they'll broadcast the coronation again, Harry? You know how they do sometimes.

Search me, he said.

I saw the Queen in Victoria, she said. She was only a princess then.

She circled her fingertip around the lid of the salt. The glass had been greased by oily thumbprints. The salt looked yellow inside.

Roy, you were with me. Do you remember?

He had been pressing his bread into a pool of gravy.

Of course.

You had barely turned sixteen. She reached across the table and cupped his cheek. —My handsome boy . . .

He sat patiently until she withdrew her hand. I thought she might smile with embarrassment, but instead she sighed. Her nails were not yellow like the salt. She had lacquered the tips.

Roy folded his bread in half and pushed it into his mouth. It reminded me of a French word I learned before school let out. *Gaver*, to force-feed. Madame Collet indicated the long neck of a goose, then mimed ecstatic choking. That's how they make foie gras, she said, which I had never tasted.

Verne reached for an egg. She saw me watching and paused. She lifted the plate and offered it to me. I took one to be polite.

Thank you, I said.

She chose one for herself. She thwacked it on the table and rolled it with her palm so the shell chipped. The fragments clung to the white's thin fabric, which she discarded on the side of her plate.

Willa, said Roy, under the voices of Irene and Harry, who were discussing something else from the radio. —How will you get home?

Verne bit the tip of her egg. She chewed slowly and swallowed.

Ride my bike? I wiped my mouth with my napkin.

Roy incised a strip off his beef and lanced it with his fork. He hovered the meat at his plate with the tines pointed down. —I could drop you off.

My mother may not be there, I lied.

He looked at me for a long time. He lifted the fork and slid the beef into his mouth.

7

AT FIRST, SHE CALLED IT a get-together. A few days earlier, she'd told Eugene she planned to have the neighbours over Wednesday night. The regular gang, you know. I suppose he asked what gang, because over the phone she said, The *gang*, Genie. Wanda and Pam. Yes, their husbands will be there. No, that one is Ko-Ko.

I lay on a towel in the grass while she recounted her plans to me and Patrick. Last month, Pamela Rice held a do with her nephew from Victoria, a barkeeper. She and her husband had returned from Cairo with a water pipe. It was a hit. No one had seen a *shisha* before. They sat on cushions on the floor and blew hoops of smoke in each other's eyes. It's all right if you can't smoke real tobacco, Mom said.

She had asked Roy to bartend. She bought limes and salt. She ordered tall bottles of gin, white rum, bourbon, tequila. Pamela and Gerald would bring their water pipe.

What about food? Patrick asked, as if interested.

We were drinking iced tea. Patrick hadn't been sitting long before he migrated to the hydrangea bush to complete some casual weeding. That gesture seemed fake to me—he didn't garden. I doubted he'd ever lifted a spade.

I thought we'd do the cantaloupe, said Mom.

He separated the globes of flowers with his hand and bowed into the opening. He combed his palms over the earth. Mom watched from her chair.

What do you think? she said. What does your mom serve at parties?

Patrick ripped a weed out of the soil. He sat back to examine the leaf, then tossed it behind him and ducked back inside the shrub. Mom stood from her chair and walked behind him. She slipped her foot from her velvet slipper and planted it on the base of his spine. He yanked out another weed and glanced at her foot over his shoulder. I watched them both, unable to move.

Sounds fine.

You weren't listening. What did I say? She kneaded her foot into his back.

He turned and her foot hung in the air.

Cantaloupe.

She lowered her heel back to the grass.

What else should we serve?

You know I'm happy with a sandwich, Aunt Dolly.

Dolly. Only Dad and Eugene called her that. My fingers screwed into the grass.

Oh hush. Tell me what you think about celery hearts.

Celery's okay.

Ducky, what do you think?

It was the first question she'd addressed to me. I couldn't answer. I funnelled my eyes at her accusingly.

Patrick walked his hands back into the garden bed. He remained enclosed this time, his hips flexing—buttocks clenching in his shorts. I remembered suddenly this was where he'd buried the dollhouse. Did Mom remember? Had he found fragments of it?

You've got a problem with aphids, he said finally. He backed out of the bush and blew a crushed insect off his thumb.

It's not a dinner or anything, Mom went on. I've always believed you should leave dinners to trained chefs. On Thanksgiving, I tried to imitate a meal we ate in Seattle and it was disastrous. You remember, Willa? Milk-fed chicken, creamed spinach, Lorette potatoes. Maybe we got the wrong kind of chicken. The potatoes were all right.

Patrick stood and walked back to the terrace stool. Soil filled his fingernails and the creases of his hands. I waited to see whether he would wipe them before he touched his drink. He did not. His finger pads left a column of black prints on the glass.

The day of the party, my mother mopped the floor for the first time that summer. She opened all the French doors and the sun blew in. The house became a wind tunnel and all the chiffon curtains sucked inside. They reminded me of whale baleen—white sheets to filter out the mayflies and summer pollens. Even in the centre of the house I could feel the sun on my skin. The breeze smelled of salt.

Mother swept around me. She held the dustpan in one hand, a small brush in the other. She had tied her hair back in a green scarf. Her lips kneaded a cigarette. A ribbon of blue smoke marked her progress across the floor. She had already cleaned the windows, and if you stepped close enough to the glass you could smell vinegar. I helped tidy the cushions on the sofa. I beat the rugs outside on the porch. The dust rose around me and I coughed. Mom emptied the dustpan into the lavender bed.

Why don't you pick some flowers? she said.

I picked lavender and filled the empty Campari bottles that had accumulated. I planted them on the dining table and windowsills, the butcher block in the kitchen and any ledge I could find. I rubbed the oil into my wrists and behind my ears, and the scent trailed my movement like my mother's smoke. In the living room, she put a record on. Her hips ticked to the beat as she dusted the mantelpiece. She had fixed herself a drink and held the tumbler in the same hand as her cigarette. She couldn't hear enough Anita O'Day that summer; I think she might have been singing "How High the Moon." The baleen blew in through the French doors. My mother sang and wiped motes off the mantel clock with her palm. Drink and sun warmed the apples of her cheeks. Nicotine cleared her eyes. She looked vital.

Darling, she said. If I give you a boost, could you reach the cobweb on the light fixture? She knit her fingers together and I stepped onto her hands. She lifted me as if I were no weight at all. A silk thread joined the fixture with the plaster. I separated it with my finger.

Good girl, she said into the backs of my knees. —Is it fun up there? She turned and whisked me in a circle through the air.

A barman from Ganges delivered the spirits. Then Roy arrived on his dumpy horse with buckets of ice. The pails did not fit in the freezer so we emptied the meat cuts and poured the ice right in. Mother marinated the celery hearts in honey. I squeezed condiments into a bowl for the shrimp cocktails:

ketchup, horseradish, lemon juice, Tabasco, salt. Patrick mowed the lawn with the eggbeater mower. We couldn't hire musicians in time, so Mother selected albums from her collection and left a stack by the record player. She offered me five cents an hour to change sides. I said okay. She said, You don't need to decide anything. I've already selected an order. I scanned each paper sleeve to peruse the lineup: Anita, Dean Martin, Frank Sinatra, Cole Porter. I slipped in Hank Williams when she wasn't looking—near the bottom so she'd be too flushed by then to tell me off. On every windowsill the lavender smelled of dopey bees.

Then, the levee—we drew a bath of Epsom salts and rosemary oil. My mother stood naked in the tub, the water branding thick cuffs around her calves. She shifted her weight uncomfortably and rubbed her shoulders. I knelt beside the tub and rinsed water over my forearms. She crouched. Heat rashed over her thighs every time her tailbone bobbed in the water. With a sharp breath, she sat and her body unfolded along the basin. She rested back against the tile. Her skin appeared smoothed rather than smooth, as though her blemishes had been dulled by cigarette smoke and pots of expensive cream from Eaton's. Her teeth were a fraction too large for her mouth, though square, trophy-like. I had my father's eyes—round and gullible. My mother had eyes like two slivered almonds.

In the bath, my mother massaged cream up her calves and stripped it with a razor. I held her hair back. She had not soaped yet. A gentle odour leaked from her armpits.

Would you like to come in? she asked. We had not bathed together since I was a kid.

Is it hot?

Not too bad.

I peeled off my socks and sat on the rim of the tub. The water yellowed when I dipped my heels in. Most days, I did not wear socks. My mother sighed back and closed her eyes. Her skin was evenly tan for a woman her age. None of her friends sunbathed without a costume. I thought of the sphinx with the head of a woman, body of a cat and bird's wings, carved from a block of stone. Outside, Patrick clattered the lawn mower back into the shed. I worried briefly he would enter the house while we padded down the hallway, swollen and ruddy from the bath, only a towel between him and our breasts.

What stands on one leg and keeps its heart in its head? said my mother. I looked at her. Her eyes remained closed.

What? I said. I pulled my dress over my head and slipped into the bath, facing her.

A cauliflower. She guided my foot into her lap and rubbed it with soap.

Joan didn't leave any party clothes here, so I made do with my own wardrobe. I wore a green and white circle skirt. I combed my hair with a side part and fixed it out of my eyes with a metal pin. Mother wore her rosé dress with a scoop neck and fitted midriff. She curled her hair in a neat parcel around her head. She looked like something you might squeeze into a drink. We had both dressed hours before the guests were due. Now we sat on the sofa in the living room, our bodies arranged lengthwise to avoid wrinkling our skirts. It was Patrick's turn to bathe. He had been in the bathroom a long time.

You look grown up, Mom said.

Thank you.

Who said I meant it as a compliment? Her eyebrows appeared darker than usual, as if she tinted them with pencil. —Kidding, she said.

Roy was outside filling a trough of water for his horse. We
both felt their absence—Patrick and Roy's. We sat like two
acquaintances whose mutual friends had gone to the bathroom. Yet we shared a basic intimacy. Our silence was toler-
able because we knew the other felt it too. And we had bathed
together. She had washed my foot.

Is that my shirt? she asked.

No.

It was a blouse I had adopted from Joan as she stopped
wearing it. I hadn't washed it and I could smell the honeyed
fragrance of her body odour and roll-on deodorant.

It's nice having you around the house, she said.

I had never left the house and didn't know what she meant.
We smiled at each other.

At six we heard an engine up the drive. It was too early for
guests. I stood from the couch and entered the dining room,
where I could see the driveway from the window. Every
movement in that skirt felt unattached from the earth, my
feet loosed from the floorboards. I could get into this role of
women who float. I expected to find Pamela Rice's Plymouth
in the drive, or even Roy's parents. I did not anticipate
Eugene's Buick, which he took on the vehicle ferry to Victoria.
He sat behind the steering wheel in his work suit and an olive
tie. Luke squirmed in the centre seat, grinning at me from
under his cowboy hat. Joan perched next to him. She opened
the door and untucked her legs from the car. She wore pale
stockings and a pleated dress, her pearl hair pinned into a roll.
She had our father's squared jaw and china-blue eyes, and in
that moment, I wished she had stayed at Linda's.

Hey, Mom?

She joined me at the window. We watched our family trail
to the house. We turned to face the front door. She didn't open

it for them, but pulled a cigarette from her carton and lit it. Eugene opened the door and stood on the mat while Luke beetled around his legs toward me. Then he too stopped short. We must have been a sight, given they had left us with unwashed hair and bare feet, Mom in her kimono, me in an onion sack. Joan paused beside Eugene, then continued over the threshold. She touched Luke's shoulder and guided him toward her.

Well I hope we're invited, she said. Her tone was breezy.

Mom blew a stream of smoke from her mouth.

I'm sorry, said Eugene. Are we interrupting?

You should have said something, said Mom.

The guests were due in an hour.

Luke removed his cowboy hat. He had acquired a string tie in Victoria, and played with the silver horse medallion distractedly. —Can I wear my cowboy hat? he asked.

Eugene half-stomped, half-limped after Mom into the living room, his bad foot sweeping the floorboards behind him. Joan and I followed. I could feel her stare roaming up my hips to her blouse tucked into my waistband. I didn't meet her eyes.

Yes, Luke, I said.

In the living room Mom stood next to a vase of tall peonies. The petals were a similar pink to her dress, and they made her appear as part of a greater apparatus—a system of plants.

Roy walked in from the back of the house. He had changed into suit trousers and a shirt that looked pressed long ago, as though he'd worn them once for a funeral, then carefully hung each item back in his closet.

Who are you? asked Eugene.

The bartender, said Mom.

My name is Roy. His eyes gravitated toward Joan. She smiled at him and looked down. I understood the courtesy of this gesture. She pretended not to notice his gaze so he could stare less bashfully. Mom had observed the same moment. Our eyes met, then slid to opposite corners of the room.

Then Patrick appeared from upstairs in grey slacks and a white collared shirt, his school's emblem stitched onto the collar. He took in Joan too, appraised her silently, as you would a sculpture in a museum.

You're involved too? said Eugene.

Patrick pried his eyes off my sister—scanned all of us, calculating who was angry at whom, which side to take. He didn't answer his father.

Are those my socks? said Eugene.

I followed his stare to Patrick's feet. He wasn't wearing shoes. I recognized them from the wash in Victoria. They were cranberry. The cloth winged slightly from Patrick's toe.

That's it, said Eugene.

That's what? said Mom.

I'll talk to the owner of the marina. Kenneth can take a week off.

What has he got to do with anything?

I came home to discuss the options with you, but you're carrying on like a deadbeat. He fixed his eyes on Roy.

A deadbeat? my mother laughed. She clutched her cigarette to her mouth and reached her other hand for the bookshelf.

Joan, come with me upstairs. I threaded my arm through her elbow and pulled her toward the stairwell. —I want you to tell me about kissing.

What? she said. Out of surprise, she did not resist. I looked back and Mom met my eyes again. Patrick's gaze followed us up the stairs.

8

UPSTAIRS IN HER ROOM with seahorse wallpaper, I sat on
the bed and Joan stood at the window without a blouse, her
arms folded behind her back to fasten her bra. Her shoulder
blades pushed from her back and made her look thin, though
she had gained weight this summer—a feminine band around
her buttocks.

What's going on? she asked as she turned to adjust the
weight of her breasts in the cups.

My own chest would never fill that bra. The cups were
pointed like martini glasses.

Nothing, I said.

Who's that younger guy?

No one.

Yeah, right. Is Mom screwing him?

I winced.

Are you?

I must have looked horrified, because she laughed.

Never mind. Stop staring at my tits, by the way. I'm wearing insets.

She changed into a red button pencil dress and white

pumps. It felt unlucky for my sister to be so devastating.

You look nice, by the way, she said. Are you wearing enough petticoats?

Hm?

Want to borrow mine? She rooted through her drawer and tossed me one of her crinolines. —Wear that instead of the taffeta, she said. It's got more pouf.

Thank you.

You look fine without makeup, but do you want me to go over your eyes?

Okay.

Only if you want.

Sure.

Sit here. I'm so jealous of your skin. She dipped her eye pencil in a glass of water and wiped it on her forearm.

At parties in Victoria, Joan and I used to dance under the stairs. Mom dressed us in frocks that tied at the back, socks folded over our polished shoes, and Joan danced smoothly, she understood how to skip her feet to the beat and sashay her hips like you see in the movies. I ran in circles with my arms stretched behind me as if I were trying to fly. Every so often I would kneel to examine a bottle cap on the floor or curtsey to one of Mom's friends, then I would take off again, zipping through the living room with my arms trailing behind me like a wake. And in summer we danced in the orchard behind our house, dirt licking the sides of our black Oxfords, my pudgy legs next to Joan's long ones. We didn't need music then.

She and I made our way downstairs, a slow-moving duo—my sister confined by her snug skirt, me by my orb of crinoline. From the stairwell, the guests of the party looked like somnolent fish. Someone had dimmed the lights, and more brightness shone from amber lamps and the horizon outside. The guests drifted through the murk, as though under a felt of warm algae. Their scales glimmered. A candelabra stood in the corner of the room. Ko-Ko wore a black and white panel dress, which matched her sunless cheeks and the stole of hair she had smoothed over her shoulder. Wanda O'Reilly wore a swollen pink dress with long sleeves. A brooch joined the two halves of her bodice. When we got downstairs I saw it was a drooping jaguar with limp limbs and a tail, as though the pelt had been shucked from the animal's frame and thrown over a curtain rod. Roy prepared drinks at a card table in the far corner of the room. He cupped a cocktail shaker and beat it up and down.

He's handsome, said Joan.

He lifted his eyes to us and raised a glass. Again, his gaze lingered on Joan. Mom stood with Eugene and Pamela's husband, who mimed how to light the coals for the water pipe. She smiled now and then at his charade, but her focus remained on the other side of the room. Roy did not return her glance, though she watched with such devotion, he must have noticed. I hadn't seen Patrick yet.

I guided Joan to the middle of the living room, where we had cleared the sofas for a dance floor, and where Wanda threatened to inveigle her husband into a foxtrot; she pressed her palms to her waist and sucked in her figure and shimmied her shoulders in such a way that was meant to be inviting. Joan dropped her hand in mine, and we stepped back and forth with half the clumsiness and energy we used to. I surveyed Ko-Ko's dress, her black strap of hair. If I studied her beauty, I hoped then, I could absorb it—I would grow longer, pointed in the right directions. Then I saw him—squatting in the corner with Luke's rock tumbler.

The tumbler had arrived in a card box last December, one week before Christmas. None of us had seen Dad since Eugene moved in, but his parcels arrived like clockwork one week before birthdays and Christmas. In his card, he said if Mom let us visit him, he would teach Luke how to use it. *In the meantime, Willa will help you read the manual.* That he'd entrusted me with the task inflated me with pride; I committed my energies to the manual last winter, reading the steps before guiding Luke through each one. Rock tumbling was a long process— each cycle required days of patience as the rocks spun first with coarse grit, then medium, then fine grit in week three, and finally polish. But after that final cycle, it was magic: the lustre unlocked their colour, so what had appeared dull on the beach opened into agate or mossy green. My favourite was striped gold and black, shaped like the heart of my palm.

Luke had recently finished a batch; the tumbler was empty. But at the back wall, where he had left the device plugged in, Patrick crammed the barrel with silty rocks from the garden.

Hey, I called. Cut it out. You'll jam it.

When I reached him, I snatched the barrel from his hands and tucked it toward my armpit.

So?

It's my brother's.

I unplugged the machine and slotted it onto a high book-shelf, placing the barrel beside it.

When I turned back, his eyelids had sunk into an even, bored plane.

I know where Mom's keeping the spare liquor, I said.

We sat outside on the porch swing, sipping from a bottle of gin. Patrick gulped swigs that sparkled down his chin. I took tidier sips. Our eyes kept chiming together in a way that made me feel warm. I knew this angle of his face well—his small ear and cheekbone, the blade of his nose. His hair had been recently clipped to his scalp, except on the top of his head, where it rose in a subtle wave.

Suddenly the lamps inside shut off—maybe a guest flicked a switch by accident. Darkness fell over the porch. I grew conscious of an even tapping, his finger on the arm of the swing. When the lights flipped back on, I was still staring at him: Eugene's socks, the school shirt with sleeves rolled past the elbows, his strong finger punching into the metal arm—and he was staring at me. A breeze wafted over us, rustling the ivy on the fence so the vines looked alive, sucking termites from the wood.

I'm cold, I said. Can we go in?

I had only taken a sip or two of gin but when I stood I could feel it, my head swayed with the motion. Patrick must have felt the same sensation because he also started to laugh.

When we returned inside, Mom stood in a circle of neighbours whose hands refracted light from their cigarettes and martinis and slits of sapphire. Luke sat against the wall in the shadow of a grandfather clock. He ate pineapple rings from a tin. Joan bent over him, coaxing him to stand.

Beside me, Eugene clapped Patrick on the back and said, You behaved yourself this week?

Like a soldier.

Eugene sucked the saliva off his tongue—releasing it in an undulating motion that wiped his front teeth. His grip tightened on Patrick's shoulder, but before he could say his usual *Don't be smart*, Ko-Ko's husband stretched his hand toward Patrick, said, This your son?

So they say.

Patrick set his mouth as they chuckled.

I'm tucking this fella into bed. Joan appeared beside me, Luke's fist clamped around the hem of her dress. With his other hand, he clawed the sleep from his eyes.

I knew I should offer to help, but I only nodded. She steered him toward the stairs. When Luke looked back at me, I mouthed goodnight.

Pamela stepped between us, blocking my view—her breasts packed into a Grecian neckline, palms filled with limes she had fetched from the kitchen. She presented them to Roy.

I approached the bar, waited until Pamela backed out into the dance floor, a drink in each hand.

Roy nodded to me and raised a glass of whatever he was sipping. —Would you like a drink?

What kind? I asked, knowing a whole drink would ruin me.

Do you like limes?

I nodded. He squeezed half a lime into a glass and stirred it with sugar and crushed mint, which he had plucked from outside. He wet the glass with white rum and filled the rest with ice and soda.

That's Cuba's drink, he said.

I accepted the glass from him and sipped. It tasted green, effervescent.

Roy, could I have a sidecar?

Mom's palm settled on the back of my neck, stroked the skin under my collar. She bowed to sniff my glass, the mist of carbonation dusting her nose. —Are you getting her drunk?

Hey, he said with a shrug. —That's Cuba's drink.

She frowned at him. Cuba had been in the headlines a lot—the president had seized back power, and there were rumblings of a paramilitary group forming to overthrow him.

Across the room, Pamela stood like the Statue of Liberty,

gripping her cocktail away from her like a torch. It reminded
me of what my mother said this summer when we were taking
a family photo in front of Eugene's yacht. She taught me and
Joan a trick. She said it would be useful one day. Keep your
hands on your hips when someone takes a photo of you.
Otherwise the flesh of your arms will bunch at your armpits.
That was the first moment I ever considered my flesh. I knew
Joan was beautiful, but I also thought of my French teacher
that way. Her armpits bunched. In the picture, Joan and I wear
white jumpers, my mother in long-waisted yacht pants, all six
of our arms bent at our hips like duck wings. Eugene printed
three copies. I buried mine in the yard.

Duck, why don't you see if anyone wants a top-up?

Roy played with a cube of ice on his scoop. The cube
shifted up and down, back and forth in a miniature cross, a
puddle sweating around it.

Willa, said Mom.

I scowled at her and left them at the bar. On the dance
floor, Pamela lifted her sternum so high she looked like a
goddess of war, levitating above them all, ready to pin them
with arrows. Eugene described to her his plans for the new
gazebo. Wanda swayed by herself in her pink dress, arms
bent like a cactus. Ko-Ko whispered into Pamela's husband's
ear, and all of them appeared so wicked and clownish, I turned
and went upstairs.

Joan sat with Luke in his bed. She looked grand in the
toy-sized frame, like a mother who hired a nanny to conduct
the cleaning and feeding, who remained bright at the eve of
a day, who read to her son *and* attended parties, clasped the
hands of strangers, took drinks and cigarettes, danced. She
would balk at that description—she always denied her mater-
nal instinct. I'm a good sister, she would say. That's all. But

here she sat, reading from a book of bedtime stories. She had a voice I liked to hear with my eyes closed. I sipped my Cuban drink and leaned back against the headboard.

Her voice paused and I felt the glass tug from my hand. I opened my eyes. She leaned over Luke's forehead to sip the beverage, then passed the glass back to me. We continued to pass the drink back and forth. After the story, Luke asked for another. I left her with the drink and went down the hall to my own room. Out the window, dark had fallen and a pale navel of moon illuminated the seafoam. It reminded me of Verne and the blue queasiness I had been feeling—an unease with the fact of her, her coolness toward me. Had I dreamed the canoe, the rabbit, the barrette?

Roy and Mother were another source of queasiness. I thought it best to ignore them. I would return to Joan and we would scavenge the cupboards for bridge mix or chocolate chips. Eugene would be in bed soon—too loud and red-faced to go on suavely. He had a keen sense of embarrassment and when to excuse himself. Mother will have fortified the corner with Roy, petting his cheek, lighting his cigarettes, passing him a tumbler for refills.

I passed Luke's room on the way back down and saw Joan had fallen asleep beside him. I waited long enough in the doorway for her to sense my presence and open an eye. She had a mother's awareness, no matter what she said—a shallowness of sleep.

Come in, she said. There's room for three.

I thought you'd be back downstairs.

She shook her head. —Should I be? Come in. You're letting in the light.

I want bridge mix.

Oh, do we have any? Don't get my hopes up.

I'm not sure. Want to come?

I'll wait here.

You'll fall asleep.

I won't. I'll stick coins in my eyes.

We played this game as children. You lay pennies or nick-els over your eyelids. Whoever woke with the coins still on her face won. It was to do with poise. The ability to control movement, even in sleep.

Don't eat all the jujubes, she said.

Downstairs, the guests were not standing any longer. They had spread themselves over the floor cushions. The men had removed their socks. Their heels were cast over the wood like pale onions. The women still wore their pumps, which made their thighs look thinner. Their limbs folded over each other in lazy bundles. I could not discern whose calves began at whose hips or knees. Mr. Tobin had removed his trousers. I should have turned away then, but I felt riveted. My mother's friends did not move with their eyes. They moved by their hands, sedately. Eugene had not gone to bed. Pamela mea-sured his long thighs with her fingernails. He clamped toward her and shuddered. Mom sat on the floor with one knee up, the other foot massaging Mr. O'Reilly's crotch. In her hand, she held the mouthpiece of the *shisha* pipe. The hose slunk over her thigh from the water bowl. She sucked in. The water bubbled. A spectre of smoke trailed from her lips. The gram-ophone played a sawdusty cello. Ko-Ko searched the creases of Wanda's knees with her nose. Someone had closed the windows and the air smelled of apple smoke; orange and ber-gamot; tequila; damp underwear; Worcestershire sauce. Pamela unbuttoned Eugene's trousers and took the weight of him into her palms. His hips pushed toward her. All of their limbs undulated to the same wallowing bass. I could not see Roy or Patrick. The moment I registered that, a hand settled on my shoulder. Patrick stood behind me, dishtowel folded over his elbow, as if he'd taken a turn behind the bar.

Where's your sister? he asked.

In bed.

Do you want to go outside?

I felt a pang of guilt, remembering the bridge mix. But I let Patrick guide me to the door. He waited on the porch while I slipped into Mom's canvas shoes. The record finished on the player. No music seeped from the open doors, no glasses clinked, no one spoke. The house was silent, but brimming over like a rush of weeds growing or tide pools filled with pulpous anemones. I took his hand and led him along our path to the sea. His palm sweated into mine.

Watch your step, he said, though I could run to the beach with my eyes closed. When he spoke, his voice fluttered before it found his usual rhythm. He was nervous, I thought.

At the shore, he continued past the high-tide mark and stirred the water with a whip of kelp.

Hey, he said. Phosphorescence.

I combed the sand until I found a flat rock, then hucked it at the water. The stone skipped three times. A fleet of bright worms peeled off each ring.

Ever swum in phosphorescence? he asked.

I shook my head.

I won't look, he said. He turned away and lifted his shirt over his head.

The muscles in his back cinched together. I rotated too, glancing behind me to check if he was watching. I unbuttoned my skirt. He unzipped his trousers. I pulled off my silk blouse without undoing all the buttons, waded out of Joan's crinoline and folded both on the log.

Still not looking, he said as he walked naked to the water.

I left my panties on. My hands fanned over my breasts to hide my nipples.

The cold would take my breath away, but I didn't wish to enter daintily, my breasts glowing in the dark like two raw scallops. I lowered my arms and crashed into the sea. The phosphorescence trailed after me. Sparks spun from my hips when I shifted to face Patrick. He dove from the shore. As his back breached the surface, blue lights poured over his shoulders, turned from his thighs. I couldn't feel the cold. He touched my cheek.

It's in your hair, he said.

When he laid me in the shallows, my heels continued to float. A wave rocked me onto my tailbone, my knees roaming to the surface from the buoyancy of salt. I laughed because the tide would not let me sit, and when I flapped for balance, sparks dripped from my elbows. Patrick lowered himself onto my hips.

Is this okay? he asked.

I nodded. Joan had demonstrated sex with paper cutouts from *Silver Screen* and the Eaton's catalogue. I understood it was something to get over with. I watched his face for clues to the shapes my face should make. He pushed my panties to one side and searched between my legs. His finger settled on one divot and flicked. His fingernail was long, but he stroked carefully, like a dentist. Goosebumps flushed up my wrists.

Is this okay? he asked again.

I nodded, but his eyes were closed. He opened them when I did not answer.

Yes, I said.

We looked at each other as he rubbed me, and another rash of feeling prickled my skin.

His hand burrowed under the small of my back and he hoisted me up the shore so I could rest my shoulders. Joan had said sex started from kissing, so I pecked the corner of his mouth. He pecked me back. Then his penis butted into the bone of my thigh. The contact startled me at first, this fifth limb. He kissed my neck. A surge of sensation unrolled between my legs. His penis butted my crease, where he was stroking, then my anus. He was trying to find a way in. I opened my legs to help, but held my breath.

Relax, he whispered.

I tensed deeper. He found a space where he could push inside. I gasped at the surprise of it.

Are you all right?

I nodded, but wanted to know how much longer this would take. The ocean had grown cold. A rock cut into my buttocks.

He sunk deeper, and I grunted at the pain, then relaxed as I saw the pleasure display across his face. His privates jangled with mine and after a few moments the impact felt less like an injury. His palm rammed into the sand above my head. His mouth waxed open, his eyes bunched in gladness, and sparks of phytoplankton hurled between our belly buttons. His mouth contorted and a groan poured from his throat. He pumped twice more and folded beside me.

I wanted to nurse him. I peeled a band of seaweed off his chest. I pressed my nose into the hollow of his collarbone.

9

I AWOKE IN MY BED with blankets tucked to my chin. A knot had formed in my back from the jar of cream, which I now felt bulging under the mattress. I whipped off the top sheet and found a spot of blood on the bed linen. Four clay fingerprints stamped my thigh.

My sister knelt on a bank of seaweed with my underwear in her palms. She dunked it under water. She rubbed the stain with a small stone.

Downstairs, my neighbours gathered their limbs and walked home with soreness between their legs. Wanda hid a salt stain with her handbag. Pamela searched the living room for her stockings and husband.

Maybe they're together? said Mom.

Pamela sucked the spit from her gums. She picked a penny off the floor.

Wanda! shouted Wanda's husband. He tripped after her with the unopened bottle of wine they had brought.

Ko-Ko sat in the driver's seat of her husband's Cadillac and peeled an orange.

Eugene lay awake in the bathtub. My mother knocked on the door and he pretended to sleep.

I know you're awake, she said.

She climbed inside the tub and passed him a mug of coffee.

No one had closed the curtains, and sun pounded through the window. When I opened my eyes, it seemed to me the walls had curved. They folded around me like the dome of a cabbage, the light translucent, filtered through veins and ribbing, the waxed cuticle of a leaf you could dip in water. My throat was parched. I wanted to drink from this leaf, to immerse the bract into a full sink. As I lay there, the walls crisped back into hard angles. Something scratched at the door. It was a gentle sound, one penny scraping the date off another penny. While I identified the origin as a teacup and saucer, someone knocked. I tugged the duvet over my thighs and waited for whoever it was to barge in as normal. No one did.

Come in, I called, my voice hoarser than expected. I cleared my throat and found even more phlegm to descale. I continued to hork as Joan nudged the door open with a breakfast tray.

I thought you wouldn't want to come down, she said. She had brought a wire rack of toast and two cups of tea.

I turned to the window, embarrassed, and focused my gaze on the embroidered curtain, the pattern of leaves you could trace with your fingers.

You gave me a scare last night—covered in mud like the creature from the black lagoon.

Sorry.

Hold this.

She passed me the tray as she sank onto the mattress and smoothed the bedsheets over our laps. When she finished, I lowered the tray. I didn't have much of an appetite, but a twisting knot in my stomach told me I must be hungry, so I opened the jar of blackberry jam and spread a spoonful on a piece of toast. Joan blew a ripple across her tea and sipped.

Kenneth's coming, she said, lowering the tea to her lap. She clasped her hands around the cup. —Eugene talked to his boss. He'll drive up and return to San Diego with Patrick.

I nodded, disappointed that Patrick was going, but sensing the disappointment was a by-product of relief. It would be too much if he stayed all summer—what had happened was spontaneous combustion. You couldn't repeat it.

I wiped a seed of jam from my finger to the crust. —You must be pleased, I said. To see him again.

You and Patrick get along, right?

I sipped my tea.

Could you distract him while Ken's here? We don't have much time. I want to make the most of it.

I looked at her—gingham pyjama shirt open around her chest bone, hair dangling inside her collar, her soft cheeks, the girlish gap between her teeth.

Besides, Kenneth might ask me something, she said, a smile brimming.

Ask you what?

She shrugged. —It's the last time I see him before he goes to college.

Outside, the last guest's car churned the gravel from the drive and rolled out. The house fell silent.

Just let Ken and me have some alone time, she said.

I lowered my toast to the tray and leaned back on the pillow, tilting my cheek away from her. Out the window, a jay hammered the trunk of a fir tree.

I have a headache, I said. I might try to sleep longer.

But it's eleven.

Just another half-hour or so.

I pushed the tray off my lap, and after a moment, she climbed from the bed and lifted it from the mattress.

Are you okay, Willa?

I'll be down in a jiff.

I curled on my side and listened to her feet kiss down the hall.

Over the next two days, no one mentioned the party. Roy did not return to the house. He had left in the night before the other guests. He wasn't there when Patrick and I crept in from the beach. My desire to see him had faded. I sensed it had for Mom as well. His absence proved she no longer thought of him, as I no longer thought of him, as if our combined wills had drawn Roy here—not hers alone, nor mine, nor his.

Patrick avoided me also, but I felt his stare sometimes at dinner, or when I emerged downstairs in my nightgown. We were cordial with each other, our interactions clipped with new politeness, full sentences, please and thank you, eyes sliding to opposite sides of the room, only watching each other when we thought the other was not looking. We sensed the other person, of course, if anything our sense of the other person had intensified, but we allowed each other that civility, to pretend not to know we were watched.

On the third day, Eugene met Kenneth at Long Harbour, where he had taken the vehicle ferry from Vancouver. I watched from the window as Kenneth's Hudson Hornet pulled into the drive. His face lifted to the house my dad built, taking it in, as if the house had acquired new meaning since his last visit.

Willa, Kenneth's here, Mom called from downstairs.

I returned to bed, stared at the wall opposite, the picture Dad embroidered during the war, when hospitalized for two months—pine cones, a sparrow nestled in the tree's young fingers. I wondered where he was now. When he would give us a call.

I didn't distract Patrick at first. I chased Luke around the garden, knelt with him on the living room carpet while he described his stamps. But the spheres of attention that circled Patrick and me—each of us sharpened toward the other person, intuiting where they stood in the room, whom they spoke to, at the same time we ignored their existence—overlapped. He sat on the driftwood rocking chair and read *For Whom the Bell Tolls*. I recognized it as my dad's copy—coffee ring circling the letters of Hemingway's name like a searchlight.

Possibly I had grown, or the water was too hot when I washed them, but my shorts felt small. The flesh of my hips pushed the hems so the fabric edged up my thighs. Patrick noticed. He noticed also the scrape on my knee from the beach. The hair I hadn't washed, which tangled down my back.

This is the 1952 migratory bird stamp, said Luke. He pointed to a stamp with two ducks, the wings of one stretched back, the other clamped forward, the sky broken with lemonade streaks.

I like that one best so far.

It's worth three cents.

I spotted Patrick's smile from the corner of my eye—at the book or Luke, I couldn't tell.

Pat told me stamps can be accepted as legal tender, said Luke.

Did he?

Patrick had tucked a white T-shirt into his slacks, a pair of sunglasses bracketing his collar, pant legs cuffed so they revealed his socks. He sat with one loafer on the chair seat, the spine of his book resting on his knee.

That's right, pal. Have you counted how much yet?

I tried. But some of the stamps aren't Canadian or American and I don't know how to score those. Luke shifted the weight off one leg to tug the sock up his calf. His hair had been trimmed to a crewcut in Victoria. Mom always let it grow to his ears.

Like this L one, said Luke. What does that mean?

Patrick leaned over his book to peer at the stamp. —That means sterling, pal. They use that funny money in England.

Oh.

Why don't you count it all up anyway, as if they're dollar signs? Or is that math too hard for you.

No, math's my best subject. I know my times tables up to twelve times twelve.

Good for you, kid, but adding's trickier—you have all those decimals. Do you have a sheet of paper? Do you know how to write three cents as a decimal?

Luke frowned at his stamps as he considered how to answer.

He's seven, I said. I don't think they've learned decimals yet.

Patrick smiled, tossing his head to shift the hair from his eyelashes. —Well I think he's smart enough. Don't you?

Sure I am, said Luke.

Why don't you ask Dad for some paper in his office. He'll help.

Luke snapped the leather binder shut. —How fast you think I can count it in?

Don't know, pal. Go for it.

He wrapped his arms around the binder and scooted out of the room calling for Eugene.

The room fell quiet again. I didn't know where to look and let my eyes fall to the patch of carpet the album had indented, as if it were still there. Similarly, Patrick returned attention to his book, but I could feel him watching me over the dust jacket.

I had begun to shift my position on the rug when he said, Your shorts are too small.

I paused, my hips raised in the air over my ankles. I lowered them back to my calves and tried to stretch the material along my thighs.

It's not a bad thing, he said.

He had lifted his hand from the book spine. Now it rested on the sunglasses at his collar, swishing the plastic arm back and forth across his chest. His eyes traced the bone of my chin, the crush of hair behind my ears, a strand wedged under the strap of my training bra, the flesh under my armpits where the bra chafed, the belly I sucked in, buttocks pressing into my heels from kneeling. Something unfolded between us— his eye on me, my acquiescence. My swelling to meet his gaze, puffing of the chest, staring at the carpet and tucking the stray hair behind my ear. I felt fullest when he watched me.

<hr>

Kenneth called it a "promise ring"—owned by his great-grandmother, a ruddy topaz flanked by two diamonds on a gold hoop, a sun-ray detail on the reverse. They would make the engagement official when he graduated from university. Joan agreed. She still had to finish high school. She couldn't wait to show Linda. *The ring's a hundred years old*, she bragged over the telephone. The band was too big for her ring finger, and she developed a tic of sliding her thumb to touch the gold to check it was still there. It was a nervous habit, this sliding and checking.

When the boys left, we followed their car down the dirt road—Joan blowing kisses, Luke chasing the rear tires, impervious to the dust that swallowed him, coating his cheeks. Eugene stood with one hand raised in salute. Mom lingered behind. We looked at each other. She pulled me in and her arm softened around my waist.

Joan boiled a kettle of water, and we drank tea on the terrace. Mom found gingersnaps in a tin. We ate carefully, our silence restorative. Instead of words, our tongues cracked brittle pieces of cookie. Joan rotated the ring to catch light, to play with how the sun bounced off her finger. Eventually, Mom excused herself for a nap.

A parcel had been placed on my pillow. It was wrapped in newspaper, *With love from P* scrawled in black ink. I closed the door behind me. The package was light, no wider than a pair of wool socks. My fingers wedged under the tape. I unfolded the paper. Inside was a floppy elephant sewn from a tea towel. The fabric felt oily in my hands. It smelled of dirt. Under the elephant, in a cradle of newspaper, sat the barrette.

GOLDEN

STATE

I learned later that Roy's aunt and uncle fostered children in Victoria—part of what would be called the "baby scoop," where infants were taken from hundreds of thousands of unmarried women and distributed among foster homes or placed for adoption. In the years after the Second World War, most of the unmarried women were Caucasian, but from the 1960s, the scoop targeted Indigenous families. Verne experienced the worst of all prejudices, I imagine—her father white, her mother from the Musqueam band in Vancouver.

My conscience still darkens when I consider that summer—how I linked her with what I found in the trees. Any resident of the islands will be familiar with boats wedged above high-tide mark. It wasn't the canoe that bothered me, but the rabbit. Imagining the task step by step. First he would have to catch the animal with his bare hands—perhaps lure her with a wheel of cucumber from his sandwich. He would clutch her in one palm, or press her belly-up to the earth, and slice her throat. With a Swiss Army knife, maybe. All the boys owned Swiss Army knives. Sawing the head would be a messy task—the knife too short and blunt to sever the spinal cord. He'd need to wiggle the blade between the vertebrae, chipping fragments of bone until the cervical spine snapped in two, eventually twisting the animal with both hands as you open a jar, separating the cartilage, muscle and arteries from her neck, then stringing the creature by her feet with twine, leaving her to bleed out. Unmotivated by hunger, without the correct instruments, it would be a gruesome task. For no audience but himself.

I never asked if he did it. Someone else might have hunted her for food; he might have found the toy and barrette by coincidence, like me. But later, after what happened, my mind would return to the rabbit strung in the tree. It had been too easy to push her from my mind. To avoid thinking the task through.

Between our first meeting in 1950 and the last in 1961, I saw him six times. Our relationship unrolled in these episodes. In the intervals between, we didn't exist. He didn't exist to me. I didn't exist to him.

10

1957

—

San Diego, California

EVERYTHING I KNEW OF California I learned when I was twelve—the blue desert, Valencia oranges, the smell of hot tires, my sister in an Orlon sweater, the woman who stole a plastic flamingo from our hotel, the surf gods, egg rolls from Fat City, sand in my swim costume, all the convertibles on Ocean Beach that parked to watch the sun duck under.

At the wedding, I promised Mom I would watch Luke. We played hide-and-seek in the garden while Patrick danced with a hazel-skinned girl from La Jolla, who attended one of those *fine Eastern schools*. The guests often spoke of the East this way—with admiration. If anyone wanted to command attention, all they had to add was "in New York" or "Long Island," or "he teaches at Yale."

I'd thought Eugene was rich, but he bore little resemblance to these people. They all spoke with their teeth clenched, and smiled that way too. They even smoked their cigarettes with gritted mouths, molars grinding saliva at the back. The women were thin. Their gemstones appeared bulky by contrast, like insects preying on their throats or licking the sweat between their fingers.

I crouched in the azaleas and watched Patrick dance. I didn't expect to feel jealous. Yet a clamminess settled into my stomach as their hips jangled, his arm around her waist—as if their twisting unpinned what we'd shared four years earlier. That was the moment I considered our time together a pinning, an experience that imprinted me at that age, that clasped me like a hand.

I'm bored, Willa.

Luke squatted beside me. He didn't even say, *You're it*. He followed my gaze toward the tent, the patchwork of guests dancing.

Shh, I hissed.

Your dress is too bright for this game.

Can't you read your comics or something?

He set his jaw. He didn't say, *Mom said you have to play with me*, like I could tell he wanted. He was eleven now—too old to play hide-and-seek. Not bold enough to make his own friends at family events. Size contributed to his shyness. He still hadn't had his growth spurt.

Okay, I said, let's go inside.

It was Saturday; *Gunsmoke* was on. I sat on the sofa and read the titles of book spines while Luke untied a shoelace and lassoed cushions. Kenneth and Patrick's mother still lived in the house. On the shelf were books like *Emma*, *Sense and Sensibility*, *Little Women*, *Great Expectations*, the Jane Austens all bound in identical cloth covers as though she had purchased a set over the telephone. None appeared to have ever been opened.

I remained this way for five minutes, until Luke settled in front of the television set. Then I slipped out of the room, returned to the tent where Patrick and the girl had been dancing.

I arrived just as her tanned shoulders followed his down the garden path. They were easy to pursue—her dress a bright tangerine, popular that season. I remained twenty paces behind them, pausing now and then to examine a flower should they turn around. He was leading her down the driveway, toward a white Chrysler Imperial—his mother's car. At first I thought he would insert the key in the ignition and drive away with her. But instead, he sat in the driver's seat, she sat in the passenger's, and they started kissing.

I couldn't turn away. I didn't even hide—I stood in my marzipan-pink bridesmaid gown, five paces away, and watched through the passenger window. I half hoped they would spot me, so they would be forced to stop.

His palm crushed her perfect side-rolls into the car seat. Their lips sawed back and forth, their hands flapping over each other's bodies, as if they couldn't find purchase. The image of insects returned to me—they were devouring each other like animals who eat their own kind. Patrick jostled the taffeta up her legs and pushed his finger inside her underwear. The expression on his face remained neutral; he looked more than anything like a dentist probing for a cavity. Which I guess he was. After ten minutes, the windows fogged over. I turned around.

At the church, Joan had worn a strapless gown with a train of tulle, but she'd changed into a cocktail dress for the reception—a champagne satin number with a neckline that scooped across her collarbone in two pleats. When I re-entered the tent, she was standing with a young man in a white suit.

There you are, she said, reaching for my hand.

Howie, this is my dear sister, Willa. Dear sister, meet Howie. A friend of Kenneth's from Cornell. You study what, again?

Chemistry.

How d'you do, I said, glancing back the way I had come, in case Patrick and the girl had re-emerged.

You care to dance?

I turned back to him with surprise. Joan squeezed my shoulder and floated to another pair of guests. I followed him onto the dance floor. He looked like a cricketer, clad all in white except the bowtie. He had black eyebrows that spanned his forehead from his temples to the bridge of his nose and shovel-shaped front teeth. His hands were oily. But he danced okay—he didn't yank me around the floor like boys at school. A caterer offered us two flutes of champagne. We downed them. My weight fell into his nicely; we shuffled with the music. I imagined Patrick admiring how well we moved—me with this older man, an Ivy League chemist. We danced two more songs before Joan cut in.

I didn't say you could hog her.

She reached for my waist as the song switched to Julie London's "Black Coffee." I let my weight shift from Howie to her. He winked and snatched another flute of champagne from a waiter's tray.

You having fun? she said.

Yes. Are you?

I'm very happy.

She looked it, a smile beating across her face. —Have you seen Mom?

Uh-oh.

She's fine.

She shuffled me around to face her. Mom had hiked her skirt to dance with Eugene. I wished, then, that Dad had made it. Last time he telephoned, he was in Hermosillo, Mexico. He wouldn't say what he was doing there. He phoned less and less now, though he still sent cards on our birthdays.

She hasn't said a word to Eveline, said Joan.

That's Eugene's ex-wife?

Mm-hm.

Then Joan pecked me on the forehead. We swayed back and forth. Neither of us led the other. We held something fragile between us, which guided our movement. I felt comforted by her warmth, her bodice damp under my palm, from her sweat or mine.

You'll take care of them, won't you? she said.

I didn't answer. The song changed. Eugene asked to dance with the bride, and I withdrew to the outer orbit of the floor. I was scanning the tent for Howie or the caterer with champagne when a hand touched my hip. Half his shirt was tucked into his cummerbund. He dropped his chin to my shoulder, in play fatigue.

Oh is it still going on? he said.

I paused under Patrick's weight, waited for him to lift his chin.

Your shirt's untucked, I said.

He touched my hand and guided us back to the dance floor.

You're awfully serious, he said.

He tapped my nose and traced the skin to my upper lip. He tapped again. I smelled a musk on his finger. A tangy, feminine musk. My eyes widened with comprehension. A smile unfolded across his mouth. He tapped again.

11

1959
—
San Diego, California

I TOOK A BUS FROM THE Santa Fe depot to La Jolla, where Joan and Kenneth lived in a white cube palace. Before the wedding, I'd never seen anything like it: a series of bleached shoeboxes designed in the thirties by an architect from L.A. I let myself in. Joan was expecting me, of course, but I wanted to surprise her. I was only there for the weekend—I didn't want to leave Luke alone for too long; he was taking exams that August to skip a grade. Patrick would be in town, I knew. I hadn't seen him since the wedding.

I couldn't help but compare our houses as I climbed the stairs. Our home in Victoria felt stuffy by contrast—even the names of its parts, like *widow's walk*, invoked thoughts of velvet and syrupy tea. Where ours was layered with ginger-bread shingles, theirs was constructed from so much bright stucco even the palmetto bugs cast shadows. Our rooms were jammed with carpets, oil ink wallpaper, bony sofas. Their rooms were cool and open, with concrete floors and windows blue with ocean. Where we had yellow-painted gables and a corner tower, they had an L-shaped roof, tiled with brick, on which a table was set with a sun umbrella. The veranda in Victoria was bracketed with cornices, a view of our crowded yard, the cedar shrubs, a crabapple. Theirs opened with an arch, palm trees, a cement path to the road.

The guest room was on the second floor, I remembered. Mom and I had slept there for the wedding. One window pointed to the sea, the other North with a view of sand, palm trees, the neighbour's property in the distance. A third window slotted above the bed—too high and narrow to see out of, but funnelling light into the room, which had reflective walls like the rest of the house. A sisal rug filled the floor between the bed and dresser.

I went in search of Joan, softening my steps to preserve the quiet—the hush you hear inside conch shells, breeze whispering over tiles, the rock of the ocean. I found her on the living room floor, staring out the glass door that opened onto a sundeck. I recognized one of Mom's kimonos pud-dled around her lap. Even in her clothes, she looked nothing like Mom—Joan's forehead wider, brassy hair curled around her ears, where Mom's had darkened and grown limp. She bent over a bowl of water with an electric fan, though the windows were open and the air felt cool inside. My shadow fell over the bowl and she turned, her eyes full. In a chaotic fluid motion, she leapt to her feet and pulled me into a muscular hug.

Willa, I'm so pleased you're here. I haven't slept a wink.

I felt a rush of affection for her and hugged her back.

Have you eaten? she said. It's early. Let's have breakfast. Do you like avocado? I can't eat enough avocado. No—I have a better idea, we'll eat out. There's a wonderful roadside diner.

None of the women from the club eat there; we'll have privacy. What news do you bring? Any boys?

She said all of this as she linked her elbow around mine and tugged me down the hall, slipping her feet into white sandals with leather straps around the heels.

Shouldn't you get dressed? I asked.

I'm wearing a top under this. I'll put on shorts. No one will be there, she repeated.

She shuffled into the room at the end of the hall, continuing to chatter as if I were still with her.

I'll wait downstairs, I called.

I relished the concrete under my feet as I padded down the steps. I paused in the dining room to roll up the light trousers I was wearing, so they appeared shorter, like pedal-pushers. I unbuttoned my cardigan and slung it over a wood chair. Then I saw him. He stood in the kitchen, glass of orange juice in his hand. His sudden physicality, yards away when I thought I had been alone in the room, made my breath skip.

He smiled as he sipped his orange juice, releasing two fingers from the glass in hello.

You frightened me, I said.

A thread of gooseflesh prickled my spine. He looked thinner than when I last saw him, but darker, his arms, face and neck tanned so evenly, the pigment might have seeped from an eroded liver. I knew it had not. He was born of the beach, like Luke. Two boys with their plastic shovel. A sea cucumber they'd scooped from the foam, hurling the gelatinous green mass back to sea.

Joan whisked down the stairs in her white shorts. —There you are, she said. Then to Patrick: When'd you get here?

Just now. Ken and I are meeting with a boat inspector before work.

It's not done yet?

He ignored her comment, restoring his gaze to mine.

Where do you work? I asked, though I knew.

A grocery store. You want to see the boat?

She can't, we're having breakfast, Joan said before I could reply.

He continued to watch me, as if she hadn't said anything.

Where will you be? I asked. Maybe we can join you after.

Dana Landing, said Patrick. Joan knows where.

Why don't we see how we feel after we eat? she said. She wiped her hand along the dining table without looking, somehow sensing her sunglasses were there, and slipped them onto her face. —Come on, let's beat traffic. The diner is a bit out of the way, I hope you don't mind. They fry the best eggs.

She locked her elbow around mine once more and guided me to the door. —Do you need sunglasses? You can borrow a pair of mine, if you like. I have a spare in the car.

Bye, Willa, said Patrick.

I glanced back as he set down his orange juice. He pulled each finger of his hand to crack his knuckles and watched us go.

Gosh, I said outside, dizzy with sun and lack of sleep. California made her faster, I observed. She talked faster. Walked faster. —You're really at home here, I said.

She gave me a half smile and checked her lipstick in the rear-view mirror. Her hands were trembling when she inserted the key into the ignition. She'd developed the tremors in high school. In public, she hid them by clasping her hands together or stuffing them in her pockets.

The diner was in a rough end of town, on the corner of two major boulevards. Even at ten on a Friday morning, the traffic slumped into town. The car beside ours had surfboards strapped to the roof rack, the car itself pink and unfurling—all the metal panels peeling off the frame. The passenger door was secured to the front seat with a bungee cord. A reflection of the surfboards crawled across the diner window as we pulled into the parking lot.

Grime mottled the pavement outside the restaurant, as if carhops regularly spilled milkshakes and hamburgers, pestling beef patties into the cement with their roller skates. Not many vehicles waited for car service, but the tables inside were packed with men in T-shirts, baseball caps, windbreakers with the collars popped. An older guy perched at the counter in a brown suit that might have fit him once but now sagged at his elbows. He read the newspaper, circling ads with a ballpoint pen. Near the entrance, a family sprawled at a table for four, the mother's hair lacquered into a blond shell, her plastic nails swiping her son's mouth, which appeared clean. Diners glanced at us as we passed. I trained my eyes on the backs of Joan's sandals.

She sunk into a booth at the back of the restaurant. I slid in opposite her. It was no use mentioning people were looking—she knew it. She opened the menu, but barely glanced at it before she searched her purse for cigarettes. She lit one with a matchbook from the china holder and blew the smoke at me through her nose.

I'm so fucking bored, Willa.

I scanned the neighbouring tables in case anyone had heard.

Oh, everyone curses here. She tapped her cigarette into an unused coffee cup. —You want to share the Hawaiian omelette?

She still hadn't looked over the menu. I closed mine and placed it back on the table.

Okay.

He wants kids, she said, as if picking up a conversation we'd had yesterday.

I emptied her cup into the ashtray. The cinders had marked a black streak on the rim. I rubbed it out with my thumb. —So?

She reached back into her handbag, digging through receipts and lozenge wrappers before finding what she was looking for. The contents rattled like breath mints when she placed the object on the table inside her closed fist. —You won't tell anyone.

No.

Not even Mom. She presented her baby finger.

I hooked mine around hers.

She opened her fist to reveal a brown glass pill bottle, the word "Enovid" on the label.

The waitress arrived with a pot of coffee. Joan flattened her palm back over the pill bottle.

She nudged her coffee cup to one side to decline. —Hawaiian omelette to share and a side of bacon, she said.

You bet, said the waitress, who looked pretty in her uniform. A red skirt bounced off her thighs. I must have looked like a high school student. A plastic headband crunched the bangs from my eyes, exposing the pimples on my forehead, the thick eyebrows Joan used to pluck for me, which I hadn't touched since she moved here.

You want anything else? Joan asked.

No, thanks.

Back in a flash, said the waitress, spiralling away in her skates.

Joan rotated the bottle between her finger and thumb, as if preparing to flick a crokinole disc across the table. —It prevents ovulation, she continued. Then her animation, which had felt forced to me, drained from her face.

I had read about Enovid—a woman had written in to the *Times Colonist* about the thousands of women suddenly claiming menstrual disorders so they could get a prescription. I still didn't know how it worked. The writer warned the effects would *imperil our daughters' morality*, but the letter was so thick with euphemisms, I flipped the page.

Are your cramps really bad?

No, you dumbbell.

You lied to the doctor?

Everyone lies to doctors. They're not ordained, you know.

They've gone to medical school.

God doesn't count medical school.

How do you know?

She slit her eyes at me. We fell silent.

Is it safe? I ventured after a moment.

She massaged her temple with the hand that held the cigarette, which grazed a strand of hair. —Kenneth doesn't know.

I followed the ember in case the strand caught fire. —What do you mean, he doesn't know?

I wanted to see how my body would react first.

She continued to mash the cigarette butt with her thumb.

First we used condoms. But after his second year of dental school he stopped buying them.

You didn't talk about it?

He's impatient. He says people are asking.

But you don't want kids?

She shrugged, tucked the pill bottle in her purse.

He must have noticed you're not pregnant.

The waitress arrived with our omelette and a plate of sudsy bacon. We cleared our glasses to make room for the dishes in the centre.

He thinks I'm too thin, Joan said, piercing a pineapple wedge with her fork.

I sliced the omelette in half, lifted a yellow slab onto my side plate.

I'm scared, Willa. What if the pills don't work? My friend Sheila got some too, and now she's pregnant. Maybe she skipped a day. Or changed her mind. I don't know.

She sipped my coffee without asking.

I reached for her wrist on the table and lay my palm overtop. I knew she didn't want me to respond with words. She only needed me to hear her—to share the burden of her secret. I bit the end of a bacon strip and sucked it in my mouth. My mind kept wandering to Patrick. How I would like to visit him at the marina—to see the yacht.

That night, Kenneth watched the news on their hideaway TV, which could be tucked back into a wood cabinet.

Hi, I said, considering whether to sit beside him on the sofa. The news anchor announced the completion of the St. Lawrence Seaway in a monotone that made me think nothing could be less interesting than the St. Lawrence Seaway—it must be the most dull of all seaways, though I couldn't name another just then. What was a seaway anyway? I thought the St. Lawrence was a river.

How are you liking California? he said.

I've always liked it, I said.

The seaway, the anchor droned, was a system of locks, canals and channels, which made me wonder, next, what was a lock, and what was the difference between a canal and a channel?

Good, said Kenneth.

When I first met him, he hovered between two age groups—
half adult, half Patrick's brother. My uncertainty about how to
treat him led me to avoid our encounters. I experienced that
stiffness acutely now.

Patrick mentioned you're repairing Eugene's yacht, I said.
When will she be ready?

Oh, there's a lot of work to do yet, he said, his eyebrows
bunching toward the crooked bridge of his nose. —She's been
wallowing in that bay for eight years.

Does Patrick help with repairs?

When he can. He works most weekends.

Is he working tomorrow?

That's right.

He reached for his drink, allowed the ice to plink in the
glass before lifting it to his lips. He had a long face, crescent-
shaped, his cheeks brown though he spent all that time back
East. He looked more than five years older than Patrick. His
high forehead made his hairline appear receded, but it wasn't.
The line had always dipped across his head with the hollows
of an M.

Say, do you have a road map I could borrow?

Sure. There's one in Joan's glove compartment.

How about a bicycle? I saw a bicycle outside.

That's my old one. It would be big for you.

But I can use it?

Knock yourself out.

12

The next day, I asked Joan to give me a grocery list. I drew a blue line from her house to the supermarket on the road map. The distance between the seat and pedals on Kenneth's bicycle made my legs plod like a deep-sea diver's in a bell suit, but I got used to it. Everyone on the street looked hypnotized: the dog-walkers, the mailman, even the pastel convertibles tucked to the curb.

The market was immaculate—a bright store with checkered floors, the shelves dizzy with labels all pointed the same way. I rarely shopped in big stores in Victoria—you could get everything you needed from the corner market. Who would eat all this? There must be twenty jars of grape jelly and twenty plastic bears of honey and twenty bottles of maple syrup. Maple syrup was not on Joan's list, but I took a bottle to test if an employee would appear to fill the hole. I added a honey bear too. Then I stuck a grape jelly where the honey bear should be and the honey bear in the row of grape jelly.

Patrick stood behind the meat counter. A cardboard display blocked his view of me—it contained stacks of cookie boxes under tented paper bunting. The sign said *Cookie Parade*

with a drawing of a clown in a ruffled collar. Nine black ele-
phants ran along the bottom of the display. I watched Patrick
through a gap in the boxes. He was serving a woman who
looked richer than Joan. Her hair had been sculpted into a
shell on top of her head with these spouts where crabs might
nestle if they didn't suffocate from her aerosol spray-net.

He spread a sheet of brown paper on the scale and weighed
two chicken breasts. He transferred the paper to the counter
and smoothed the breasts one on top of the other, folded the
paper over and tucked in the sides. He passed the parcel to
the woman and she turned, her pumps clicking toward me
along the linoleum.

When I glanced back at Patrick, he was watching me
through the gap in the cookie boxes. I jumped.

Are you hiding from me? he asked, loud enough for the
woman to hear.

No.

I approached the meat counter and directed my gaze
toward a length of salami in the case. Joan had not written
salami on the list either.

What are you doing here? he said.

The smock was too big for him. He looked like a boy
dressed as a ghost. But a tanned ghost with eyes like two glass
fishing floats. His apron was smeared with meat juice.

Joan gave me a list, I said.

Does she want salami?

No.

I fished the list from my pocket and flattened the paper
against my palm. —Figs, I said.

You won't find those at the meat counter.

I guess not.

You want me to show you?

Okay.

He thwacked off his gloves and came out from behind the glass case. He probably wasn't supposed to leave the counter unattended, or to visit the produce aisle with blood on his apron, but I didn't object.

Figs are funny, aren't they? he said as we walked. —Do you know where the word "sycophant" comes from?

I shook my head. I didn't even know what the word "sycophant" meant. His shoes were distracting me. The wood soles clacked across the linoleum more sharply than the woman's pumps. My sandals padded in silence.

It comes from the Greek *sykophantes*, he said, which means "who shows the fig," a vulgar hand gesture.

We had reached the Mission fig case. He cupped one in his palm, which had not touched the chicken directly, but maybe he should have washed his hands. The fruit looked intimate to me—its soft weight in his palm, skin the purple of blood pooling. He touched the fig to his chin before he bit. Another employee pushed a tray of bananas into the aisle. I stepped away to scan the artichokes, but Patrick stayed where he was. He lifted the hand with the half-eaten fig and waved.

When the employee passed, Patrick rammed the rest of the fig in his mouth.

How many do you want? he asked, the seeds wedged between his teeth. He flicked a plastic bag from the roll and began tossing figs inside.

I don't know, I said. The list didn't specify a number. —Seven?

You want artichokes too? He tore a second bag and began filling it with the green globes.

Okay.

Take them, he said, handing me both bags.

I set them inside the basket.

No. I mean *take them*. He wagged his middle and index fingers upside down to indicate a walking man. —Outside.

Without paying?

Who will notice?

I looked around. The employee who'd passed was restocking bananas at the bottom of the aisle.

Is this a trap?

He slung his arm around my shoulder and walked me toward the front of the store. —What else is on your list? Do you like chocolate? We sell these bars imported from Switzerland.

We were approaching another display: a fibreboard cutout of the Alps rose above a pyramid of chocolate bars. Patrick slid one off the top.

See? he said. The bar was wrapped in gold card. He tapped it against his mouth.

You ever wonder if we're twins? he said.

His tone remained even. He stared beyond me in the distracted way he often did. This time, at the Alps.

That's a funny thing to ask, I said. We have different mothers.

So?

He reached for my basket and guided me to release it into his hands.

I've been learning about twins in my psychology class, he said. When a mother gives birth to one child, her gaze finds her newborn instinctively. But in the case of twins, there are two faces. Two sets of eyes. Which one does she look at?

Both of them?

You can't split your gaze. Not evenly.

We walked toward the front doors. He spoke in a gentle voice. —So her gaze slips to the twin most aligned with her looks or temperament. Even if she imagines the resemblance. The other child is the shadow.

We were outside. He slid the artichokes, figs, maple syrup and chocolate bar into my backpack.

But we have different mothers, I said again.

He rested the pack against my ankles. —You're distracting me, he said. You'll get me in trouble.

But you're the one—

He raised his finger to his mouth. —Later, 'gator.

He glided back inside the store, the wire basket swinging from his arm.

I had leaned Kenneth's bike against the wall of the supermarket. I returned to it now, the pack sagging from my elbow. I slung it over my shoulder and walked the bike out of the parking lot. As I lifted my leg over the seat, I saw Joan from the corner of my eye. She weaved between the cars in white shorts and Mom's kimono.

There you are, she said.

What are you doing here?

Picking you up.

But I cycled.

We'll stick the bike in the trunk, she said. I have an idea.

I didn't get everything on the list, I said.

That's okay.

What's your idea?

We'll visit Sheila.

But it's dinnertime.

So?

We can't drop in unannounced.

Says who?

Joan.

Don't you want to see her house?

No.

It's ten minutes from here tops.

We left the convertible at the market. I followed her to the main road. After two blocks, we turned onto a street named after an oil like rapeseed or canola. The sun began to set as we walked into another neighbourhood with trim squares of grass and clean cars. Date palms reared from the yards, the fronds more thready and sinister than the trees along the boulevard. A knot of shadow scuttled across the road—maybe an opossum. Joan told me more about Sheila as we walked: her palatial garden with flowers like pink honey cakes, orange trees.

She could stand in front of a disembowelled coyote and still look like a wife from the Sears catalogue, she said.

Walking with my sister like this, in secret or daring, reminded me of an incident when I was seven, in Victoria. We had trespassed into a house roped off by police—the windows boarded with planks of wood, which called to mind bandages wrapped around somebody's eyes, effacing that essential part of them. Behind the planks, a window was broken, and we slipped through, a fragment of glass slicing my knee. Today a scar still sickles my kneecap. The hall smelled of body odour and feces, the air thickening as we approached the kitchen, where coils of dog poo scattered the tiles. I had never seen a home like this, the plaster blotched with damp, maybe urine, cups in the sink lined with fetid tea and cigarette ash, tins of beans rusting on the counter. The walls represented a cage, not a shelter, and that realization changed me. I couldn't shake the impression we had violated a sacred space. The house wasn't in our neighbourhood: I knew nothing about the man who lived there. But I felt certain we had defiled him.

Despite the anxiety in my gut, I followed Joan down the street. I felt stronger with her by my side—part of some larger organism. We strode hand in hand down this street named after oil. The air smelled of fried garlic and oregano.

It's the next one, she said.

The houses grew in size and splendour as we walked. The one she stopped at was a Victorian like ours at home, though much grander—painted butter yellow with a frieze of detail under the cupola, the cornices above the front door carved with sunbursts. Under the bay window, they had raked a strip of garden that grew prickly pear and kettles of sage, and in the next bed, a mass of greedy dahlias. The light in the window was on. I searched for movement or a shadow, but it was useless from that angle. Joan cut across the lawn and stepped into the window garden bed, picking her way over paddles of cactus. She stopped at the edge of the window and pressed against the wall. My heart beat in my throat. I expected the door to swing open any moment. I inched after her along the shadow of a tree. The prickly pear snagged my shorts. I paused to unhook myself and the thorn pricked my thumb. Joan squatted under the window and couldn't see a thing. I was distant enough to catch the silver light of a TV against the wall. I rose higher onto my knee and spotted a woman at a long table, her hair dyed a sherry tone. She wore a thick gold coil necklace that circled her throat like a snake, widening into a heavy pendant on her breastbone. She did not watch the television, which continued to rinse the wall in sterling light. A bowl of what look like tapioca pudding sat beside her elbow.

Is she there? asked Joan.

Let's go.

What's going on?

She's reading.

Wait till you see the backyard.

She stepped over a cactus and led the way around the side of the house.

I didn't feel as guilty when I saw how much money they must have. The lawn was dotted with Italian cherub statues. Fleshy begonias circled the grass, which was shaded by a pergola at the back. A mass of trumpet flowers wound through the wood lattice and gave the impression of life, as if the plants were expanding and contracting with oxygen.

Can we go now?

Joan pressed her face against the back window, stepping away only when she breathed a cloud of breath onto the pane, obscuring her view.

She announced the pregnancy at our bridge club, she said. You should have seen their faces. *Simply* marvellous, Doris said like a twit. How can you be *simply* marvellous?

I rested my palm on Joan's back and guided her toward the front garden. When we reached the stone path that led to the driveway, she said, Let's knock on her door.

Joan.

Five minutes.

She jogged up the front steps and rapped the door with her fist. A housekeeper answered almost immediately. She recognized Joan and showed us into the dining room, where the elegant woman sat with her book. Her hand-block print dress appeared to me expensive yet understated—something you'd overlook until you saw it in *Vogue*.

Joan, said Sheila, glancing at her wristwatch. —Am I expecting you?

No, and we won't stay a minute. I wanted to introduce you to my sister, Willa. We were just around the corner.

I was annoyed at her for using me as an excuse, but curt-sied. The gesture felt ridiculous in my shorts.

Sheila's gaze lingered on our thighs. —Have you been to the beach?

No. Ken and I have been at the marina all week. The yacht will be seaworthy soon. Once we replace the engine.

How nice, she said, before turning to me. —It's wonderful to meet you, Willa. You'll stay for a drink, won't you? Ginger ale okay?

We'd love a ginger ale, wouldn't we, Will?

Sheila smiled, but made no move to stand.

Where's Ned? asked Joan.

He golfs late Saturdays.

Ah.

A silence followed. I wanted to fill it. I considered compli-menting her garden, but realized all gardens must thrive here. San Diegans didn't even talk about the weather unless it rained.

Still no one spoke.

Your dahlias are thriving, I said.

In truth, dahlias disturbed me—the perfect spheres, open-ing in hundreds of symmetrical cells, like an alien apartment block. Or worse, mouths tiered on top of each other, pristine tongues snapping from each fluted lip.

Isn't she sweet, said Sheila.

Willa's starting college this September. Aren't you, Will?

Yes. I hope to study classics.

How nice, said Sheila. We have the Brontës on our bookshelf.

I mean Roman classics.

Oh. We have those too.

You do? Which ones?

You'll have to ask Ned.

She still hadn't stood to fetch the ginger ale or invited us to sit down.

Big news, huh? said Joan. Congratulations again.

Sheila lowered the book to her lap and spread her fingers over the spine. —Thank you.

You know what I'm going to ask, said Joan.

Sheila smiled faintly, stroking the spine of the book. I sensed she wanted us to leave, and I glanced at Joan, who ignored me.

The pills. Did you stop?

Sheila's eyes flicked to me. When I met her glance, she smiled uneasily.

Oh Willa doesn't matter, said Joan. Anyway, if the pills don't work I should know.

I clasped my sister's wrist, as if to hiss in her ear, though I addressed Sheila instead. —I'm sorry, Mrs. . . .

I curtsied again, in spite of myself, and tugged Joan toward the doorway.

They work fine, if that's all you want to know.

Shei, I want to know whatever you'll tell me.

Ned will be home soon. If you don't mind, I'll see you out. She rose from her chair, and the edges of her shoulders speared past us into the hall. Joan hastened after her, and I followed, faintly stunned, uncertain if I should apologize again. We stepped onto the porch. I turned to wave, but Sheila had already shut the front door.

Joan descended the steps and stomped across the lawn, kicking grass where she shouldn't, muddying her toes. She paused below a streetlamp, unlit cigarette between her lips. Her fingers couldn't grip the match because they trembled so much. I cupped my hands around hers to steady them. Eventually, her tendons released into my palms. She bent to light the match.

Witch, she said as she whistled a stream of smoke through her mouth. I hugged my arm around her hip. We walked back to the car.

That night, at the house, I found her on the veranda, scribbling into her diary. I was about to turn around when she reached her hand for me.

Stay, she said. I want to show you something.

She set her pen on the armrest of the chair and fanned the pages back. She opened to a newspaper article she had pasted onto a blank sheet, the edges folded so they would not wing out from the cover and tear.

What is it? I asked.

She passed me the diary. The story was about an incident that occurred that year in Washington State. That was the word Joan used. "Incident." In the incident, a mother of five children drowned her youngest in a bathtub.

The article said she had sunk into a bad depression with every birth. She asked to be sterilized after the third—she couldn't bear more pregnancies and she knew it. But the obstetrician discouraged her, said she would feel better in a few weeks. The husband promised to get a vasectomy, but he never got around to it. Like he never got around to oiling the door hinges or rewiring the TV set so the picture didn't slur. All reports—from schoolteachers, neighbours, the pastor—confirmed the children were well cared for. When she recovered from labour, she devoted herself to them. But after the fifth child, the ligaments that fastened her mind together released.

That would be me, Joan whispered as we sat outside, our deck chairs facing the waves, which feathered toward us as the tide drew in. She folded the edges of the clipping back inside her diary.

Nonsense, I said. You will make a wonderful mother when you're ready.

She shook her head. —Mom has it too, she said. You don't. You got away lucky.

13

Slung between the pillars of the boat hoist, *Greta* looked ungainly—sixty-two feet in length, sixteen across, the hull itself nearly eight—like an island pried from the earth so you see its undercarriage. It felt rude somehow, witnessing the parts that sliced through water. Patrick told me she was built from B.C. Douglas fir. When the Central American treasure-hunting expedition failed, she picked up other work—fishing, guano, cameos in silent films. I still didn't understand how Eugene came into such a vessel, or why he left it there to rot. I guess it wouldn't be the first expensive item he abandoned in California. There was the house. His ex-wife. He probably wouldn't talk to his kids if one hadn't married Mom's daughter.

Kenneth worked with his shirt off. He scraped the algae from the sides, chiselled the decay. The muscles purled in his shoulders as he filled a hole with resin.

It doesn't look seaworthy to me, I said to Joan from the pavement.

It will be. Once they replace the engine.

How much does one of them cost?

Less than a new yacht, I guess.

While Kenneth worked, Patrick clambered onto the tire of the boat hoist and tossed himself onto *Greta*'s stern. Yards above us, he removed a handkerchief from his shorts and wiped his hands. No one scolded him, though the yacht hung over the concrete yard, and he could slip and splinter his head open or get strung up by the hoist's chains.

Hey, Patrick, why don't you show me the beach? I called.

He tipped his arms overhead as if to dive off the yacht, then smeared his jaw open to mimic the impact and let his arms wilt above his head, which had dropped to one side as if his neck had snapped. Neither Kenneth nor Joan took any notice.

Guano, he told me, is seabird shit, valued by farmers for its high nitrogen, phosphate and potassium content.

The tide was out. We were walking along the sand at Mission Beach. He had bought me a soft-serve ice cream from a truck on the boulevard. It smelled sour, of milk not cleaned from the machine. No matter how fast I licked, pearls unlatched and dripped to my wrist.

Cave bats too, he said. It's lucrative.

The shit.

Yes.

We had left Joan and Kenneth at the marina. Patrick's funny mood continued. He strode faster than I could with my ice cream, then turned suddenly to face me. A cloud of sand lifted as I tripped to a halt, my nose inches from his throat. He smelled of talcum powder.

You still swim? he asked.

Sure.

You could dive too. I remember that.

We were silent.

I don't have a swim costume with me.

Me neither, he said.

The beach was busy but not packed. Behind us, an egg timer dinged and a row of women rolled onto their stomachs. Down the sand, surfers had erected a fortress of red boards. A girl chased her brother with a pail of water, and for an instant I missed Luke—wondered if he was still studying, or if his friends had persuaded him to fish on the gorge. God knows, Mom wouldn't stop him.

Patrick and I walked in silence. Ahead, a woman rubbed oil on her calves. Her boyfriend tossed a football in the air, caught it idly with one hand. In the water, a girl my age floated on a surfboard, her feet kicking the tide, waves rocking her forward. Then all my fancies of California flooded back— the gold beating bodies, svelte palm trees, not one hair of cloud in the sky, which enfolded everything in sonorous blue.

It's really nice to see you, I said.

He didn't turn his head, but I could tell he was smiling. Then he stopped short again and grabbed my hand.

Your ice cream is melting, he said.

I could feel the cold beads rolling down my knuckle.

I presented my fist, daring him to lick it. He leaned nearer, his stare holding mine. Then his tongue darted and struck the heel of my palm.

You want the rest? I asked.

Something stirred in me when he took my ice cream and guided the entire cone into his mouth. He reached for my hand to wipe the cream with his handkerchief when something caught his eye. His fingers clamped my wrist and he steered our path to the shoreline. He knelt abruptly, forcing me to stoop over him, and dipped my fist in the tide. He removed a Bakelite nail brush from his pocket and pried my hand open under water. The bristles jabbed under each nail as he slid the brush over my fingertips. I stared at him, too stunned to pull away, the brush nipping the sensitive skin at the end of each finger.

After a moment he started back toward the boardwalk. I followed at a distance, tucking my swollen fingers inside my pocket, scared to check whether the sunbathers had seen. The cotton of his white T-shirt was translucent from patches of sweat. When we reached the marina, I saw damp had also spread across his thigh, where he'd replaced the brush in the pocket of his shorts. In my own pocket, a hot moistness fell from my index finger.

⸻

That night, I ventured into the kitchen while Joan tore lettuce with her bare hands for salad. It looked satisfying—this wringing of leaves, water spraying her arms as the spines ruptured. A cast-iron pot sputtered on the stove, steam dislodging the lid with bursts of moisture.

Can I help?

She had changed into blue cigarette trousers, an embroidered apron around her waist. I had never seen her cook in my life.

Could you turn that burner down? she said.

She wiped her palms on her apron and shifted to the cutting board, scooped a handful of cherry tomatoes from a paper bag. She sliced each tomato in half and tossed them in the bowl with the salad. I found the right dial on the stove and rotated it down.

I'm heating the cassoulet from last night, I hope that's okay.

What kind of casserole?

She smiled, wiped her hands once more on her apron. —It's a French stew.

Ever since their honeymoon in Paris, she deferred to France in her lifestyle—ordering ballet flats from the Champs-Élysées when she could buy them here, subscribing to *Marie Claire*, which she left stacked in the guest bathroom.

Pour yourself a drink if you want, she said. There's lemonade and Coca-Cola in the fridge.

We rarely had Coca-Cola at home, so I opened a bottle, hovered it under my nose to feel the gas spritz my lip.

She started talking again about the yacht repairs. —It's not just the cost of the engine, she said. They would have to pay for installation. Kenneth can't do that himself. Do you know how much an engine weighs? And they have to haul out the old one.

Somehow more sand had wormed inside my thumbnail. I stopped listening to Joan and focused on sucking the grains between my teeth. He had carried a nail brush with him—how long had he wanted to do this? I clenched the dried blood in my fist so Joan wouldn't see. The bristles had opened the cuticle of my index finger. Then I noticed she had stopped mixing the salad and stood rotated to me as if she'd asked a question.

Sorry, what?

Did you have a nice time with Patrick?

I searched the kitchen window for something else to comment on. It sounded so minor when I worded it to myself. *He tried to clean my nails.* Ahead, two seagulls collided above the porch umbrella. They did not screech like most seagulls wrangling over a crust of bread. Maybe they were mating. It looked violent—the whole sex act a theatre of impaling, the stronger sex goring the other with his knife.

He bought me an ice cream, I said.

That's nice.

I closed my eyes to feel the last prickle of carbonation on my lip.

Do you like him?

He's okay.

You can tell him to back off, you know.

I've had boyfriends before, Joan. I know what to do.

He's your boyfriend?

The blood flushed my cheeks. —That's not what I meant.

So he bought you an ice cream, she said. What else?

I shrugged. —He did something strange.

How so?

He cleaned my nails.

I didn't tell her how, exactly. That he pried my fist open under water, pressed the bristles so hard the skin broke. As I replayed the scene to myself, I started to question details—maybe he hadn't scrubbed so hard. Maybe he caught a hangnail. Or the whole episode was a joke. A bizarre joke, one I didn't get, but he'd always been unusual.

What do you mean?

Never mind. It sounds silly now.

Did he say they were dirty?

He had a nail brush. I don't want to talk about it.

She paused, knife poised above the cutting board. —Maybe he developed an aversion to germs at college. Those places are cesspools.

It doesn't matter. Shall I set the table?

She pedalled her knife through a cucumber. —Sheila's aunt had a germ phobia. Oh it sounded awful. They had to tether her to the bed so she wouldn't wash her hands in Clorox. The skin pimpled off her bones like a sunburn.

She glanced at me for a reaction. I bent to remove three plates from the oven.

Probably the whole thing was a joke, I said.

After dinner, I sat on the windowsill of the guest bedroom and gazed at the night between the palm trees. I would take the train home tomorrow, and the thought made me uneasy. I could feel the future encroach as a shadow encroaches on a day when you spend every hour outside and fail to notice the sun slipping below the horizon. At college, I would study Latin and classical literature—but to what end? My friends had enrolled to meet husbands—two were engaged already. I wasn't like them. More and more, it fell on me to prepare dinner, to help Luke with his homework, which he completed while I worked through my readings in the kitchen. It was crucial to me that we both secured the highest grades: to prove we were different from our mother, that we had some claim on goodness, which she had rejected for herself but which she could not damage in us. That was how I perceived it. *Goodness* would elevate us from the house in Victoria, from the island. But at what point, exactly, would my grades convert to freedom? Ninety percent for an essay on the relationship between madness and blindness in *King Lear* would do me as much good as sixty if both futures required a husband. Less good, if I continued to decline dates.

Did Patrick want a wife?

I reached for the backpack on the floor and removed the bar of chocolate we stole. I rearranged myself on the sill, legs folded outside. The palms looked spidery in darkness. The nearest one was shaggy, the fronds peeling from the canopy to form an undercarriage. I read that's how they grew—as old fronds sag, new leaves sprout from the top, and the trunk elongates, leaving tracks of scars around the stem, or a hairy underbelly, which reflects the live fronds as if separated by a pool of water. On one side the fronds arced from the canopy like fingers spread to let in sunlight. On the other, they drooped and grew brittle, rustling like parchment. The shaggy palm contained this duality, life on one side, death on the other, the two halves separated by a line that receded as the trunk grew taller, sturdier, and so like us, the older the trees grew, the more dead years they dropped behind them. Unlike us, you could see the trajectory, the lived years, the fronds bracketing around the trunk like a layered skirt, until they clacked off onto the pavement. The second tree was much neater, the trunk reedy and smooth, dead fronds wrapped in a parcel under the canopy—or were those new fronds? I couldn't tell.

I opened a hole in the foil wide enough to snap off a triangle of chocolate. I sucked the morsel until it softened on my tongue.

Maybe Patrick was on to something. We were twins. I had shadowed Joan all this time. He had shadowed Kenneth. The funny thing about shadows is they absorb each other. You can't see where one ends and another begins.

GRETA

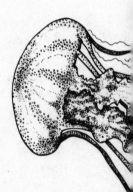

In July 1961, Joan invited me to go sailing. I had completed my second year at Victoria College. Patrick had finished his fourth at Cornell. They planned to sail her down the coast of Baja California, or as far as they could over the holiday. Fourth of July was a Tuesday, but Kenneth had booked the whole weekend free. Joan paid my train fare.

I remembered the schooner they owned—the yacht, I would call it—how I might look on the deck of their yacht. How it would feel to dive into slippery water. I imagined us eating breakfast, two couples with Pacific-tanned cheeks, orange juice on the table. How jealous my best friend would be in Victoria—even if she had a steady boyfriend who proposed regularly and zipped her up island in his MG. I would come back tanned, pimples smoothed from salt.

I called her to say I was taking the train to visit my sister in California, that I would spend Fourth of July weekend on my brother-in-law's yacht. Lucky you, she'd said. I don't have any sisters who marry rich men with yachts. Then she told me her boyfriend knew a secret spot to watch the Dominion Day fireworks. He was taking her in the MG, she might let him keep going this time.

She didn't know I had let Patrick "keep going." But I didn't feel prepared by our time on the island that summer. If anything, I felt more chaste. My belly had stayed hard. If it's so easy—if a man need only breathe the wrong way, and I'd let him erupt inside me—I must be good. I didn't realize, at first, you needed to bleed.

I didn't think about that night too often. I thought about the week we met the brothers when I got stung by the jellyfish. Later that evening, after Eugene had struck his knuckles with a belt, Patrick came to my room. I was lying under my bed, reading Nancy Drew with Dad's Kwik-Lite flashlight. Patrick crawled under the bed with me. When he straightened his legs, his feet poked from the end of the bed frame, but when he bent them, his kneecaps pushed the wood slats. I closed my book. He reached for my flashlight and switched it off. We lay in silence. When I tried to slide out, he found my hand and pressed my wrist to the floor. He said: Are you my wife? I told him I didn't think so. I tried to pry off his fingers. After a while, he relaxed his grip. I breathed in hot air that smelled like corn from his mouth. Eventually it started to feel nice, like we were holding hands.

When I think of us in 1961, before we launched the yacht into the water, an image returns to me: my sister in shorts, opal earrings that greened in sunlight, me with trousers hiked over my knees, two bronzed boys rinsing the hull with water, all of our palms pressed to the wood, as if feeling for a pulse.

14

1961

—

San Diego, California

It would have made a nice picture: the boys' shirts folded on a cockpit bench though the sun had barely pushed into the horizon, their abdomens knitted as they yanked the halyard, a great bank of canvas hoisting into the sky, the sisters watching from the foredeck, the one tall, a chamomile blouse tucked into the waistband of her shorts, the other small, dark hair undulating in the breeze that mounted as the yacht putted into the bay.

We had arrived that morning with paper cups of coffee from a roadside diner. Patrick met us at the marina parking lot and the four of us trekked the cooler and food boxes to the dock, duffles slung over our shoulders or swinging from hands, piling them on the walkway with the cans of motor oil and life preservers. Joan and I packed the items below deck, tucking food into the galley lockers in containers, so if we opened a door while under way, tins of tuna wouldn't slash out and clobber our heads. There were five cabins—two doubles at the stern, by the engine, two singles at the bow, and a double amidships, in front of the galley. Joan chose one of the doubles at the stern for herself and Kenneth. Patrick had already settled into the middle cabin, so I selected one of the singles at the bow. The berth was narrow, more like a bench, with wood cabinets underneath for my clothes. But I didn't mind feeling the edges of things. I had a large porthole.

We watched in silence as the boys tugged lines and hoisted more sails into the air. I studied their motions. I wanted Patrick to see me raise a sail on my own. To show him I knew the names of things. I had started to memorize certain terms: *spar*, *bowsprit*, *jib*, *boom*. The sounds hung in my mouth, severed from the object they represented, as when you learn any language. Each corner of the sail had a name, for example, and to remember I shut my eyes and imagined the right triangles in Luke's geometry text. *Head*, *tack* and *clew*. The head was easy—that was the top corner—the tack and clew I confused. As for the sides: the bottom of the sail was called the "foot," the forward edge, the "luff," and the hypotenuse, if I may call it that, the "leech."

I took a particular interest in Kenneth's nautical chart, which reminded me of the charts Dad had pinned to the wall at the beach house. I knew a bit on how to read them. I noted the water depths, coastal landmarks and buoys, so we could track our progress toward Ensenada. Every now and then, Joan said something to me as she watched the boys, but her voice was absorbed by the whipping canvas. Then Patrick tightened the main sheet, the sails filled, and we cut across the bay with only the creak of the boom, water rinsing the sides and the sound of air swelling into cloth.

Eventually, Joan opened the latest *Marie Claire* and I folded myself onto a cockpit bench with Kenneth's binoculars. We hooked out of the bay and drifted south, passed the Old Point Loma Lighthouse. Beyond Point Loma, the high-rises of downtown lifted into view, a grubby ivory colour against the harsh white of the lighthouse. But I found them pleasingly grubby, as if seen through a sheet of warm gauze. And beyond the skyline, scabby hills, so unlike the wet, green mountains I was used to.

After the first hour we fell into an uncertain rhythm—Kenneth and Patrick hovering over the helm, fearful the other would take over, occasionally trimming a sail to prevent it from luffing, Joan flipping through her magazine a second time, me leaning over the side of the vessel, watching the wake we lay behind us. The hours since I'd arrived in California had slipped by rapidly. I imagined it like dropped knitting, the yarn unwinding across the floor before the momentum faded and the ball rocked to a halt. What now? What did you actually *do* on a yacht? I'd brought Ovid's *Metamorphoses* and *The Old Man and the Sea*, which I had to read for my only modern literature class in September. Starting that year, Victoria College would offer bachelor's degrees under guidance from the University of British Columbia. I had decided to stay on, unlike most of my friends, who graduated that summer with a diploma. But I couldn't read on the boat—an anxious energy thrummed through me. Patrick had barely glanced at me all morning. At first I thought he was distracted with getting under way, but he had time now, didn't he? I left the binoculars on my chair and practised walking from one end of the boat to the other, arms out for balance, as we heeled to one side. I wondered, not for the first time, why Eugene hadn't sailed the yacht to Victoria. He could have found mooring space in Oak Bay. Did it mean he was planning to come back here? With Mom or without her?

When I reached the bow without stumbling, I looped back to the boys at the helm.

How's it all going? I asked.

Patrick shaded his eyes and gazed over my shoulder at the water. Kenneth grinned at me and clapped his palm on my arm.

Isn't she a beaut?

Yes. She's built from trees very near where I'm from.

Is that right, he said, his tone polite but disengaged.

Would you like more coffee? I said, staring at Patrick.

I'd love a cup, thanks, Will, said Kenneth.

Patrick nodded once at me. I turned for the companionway steps.

Joan had packed one of those Italian moka pots, similar to one we used to bring camping, so I knew to fill the basin with water and spoon coffee into the metal filter, then tighten the upper chamber so the coffee didn't bubble out the sides. I had been bracing myself against the counter with my hip, but when *Greta* pitched to the other side, I lurched into the stove, which itself was gimballed so it stayed upright. I lowered myself onto the settee and focused on a grain of sugar on the table to avoid feeling sick.

I waited for the coffee to chortle, then splashed it into four cups, which I carried painstakingly up the companionway steps on a breakfast tray. Kenneth had left Patrick at the helm and was trying to lift Joan off the bench. She stood without his help and stepped onto the deck. He followed her, slinging both arms around her waist. She leaned away from him, lay her hands over his and separated them from her hips. I pressed my knee into a bench to steady myself and waited for them to reach for their coffees so I wouldn't have to manoeuvre the tray over the cockpit coaming. Then I joined Patrick at the helm.

Thanks, he said, when I passed him the mug.

You're welcome. I cupped mine in both palms, inhaling the scent of roasted beans, allowing it to calm my nerves, scanning my nails without meaning to for grains of dirt.

Do you want to try steering? he asked.

Oh, may I? Will you show me how?

He downed half of his coffee—it had cooled from the breeze—and set it on the bench. It began to slide. I grabbed it in time and set it on the deck, where it remained stationary, though angled. He took my coffee, which I hadn't finished, and placed it beside his. Then he stood behind me, guided my hands onto the wood spokes of the wheel, and tightened his palms around my fists. He pushed gently to the right, and I felt my hands take the weight of the boat, which began to point starboard. Then he guided my hands toward the left, just a hair, and we resumed our course. He stood so close behind me I could smell the oils from his skin, the coffee on his breath, which tickled my ear. He tightened his grip over my hands, encouraging me to massage the wood, and then I felt him from behind, or I thought I did, a hardness prodding my tailbone. I resisted the instinct to flinch away and chose to relax into his hips, which pressed against me. After several long moments, he stepped back. I lifted my cup from the deck, passed his also, training my gaze on the blue ceramic rims. When I raised my eyes to his, he smiled—at my calm or his arousal, I couldn't tell. For a long time, neither of us blinked.

Willa, called Joan. Dolphins.

I stepped away from Patrick and strode toward my sister near the bow. When I reached her, the dolphins had dipped back under, but I studied the water with great concentration to avoid glancing back at him. The animals crested again a few minutes later, thirty yards from the boat, two dorsal fins carving the waves like teaspoons slicing through melon.

I felt pleased with my new swim costume—peach coloured with buttons down the bust and a low back. When I tested it at Cadboro Bay, the boys had noticed. One hauled me in the water and dunked my head. Even my best friend's boyfriend looked. I'd felt nervous about my breasts at first, whether they would slip from the sides. But so far everything remained tucked.

As the sun roasted higher in the sky, I arranged myself on a cockpit bench beside Joan. She wore a dusty-blue two-piece that exposed her midriff. I rolled onto my stomach to emphasize the cut of my own suit. The knit tulipped my bum. Sun spooled across my shoulders. Kenneth was back at the helm, and Patrick was sitting cross-legged on the aft deck. His eyes followed the sun down my spine, to where the nylon cut across my buttocks, down my legs, which goose-pimpled. Then my foot started to cramp. I tried to wriggle my toes without disturbing the stillness of my posture. Finally, I pressed my foot on the bench to relax it. I removed my sunglasses and lay back down on my stomach, nestling my nose in my forearms. I glanced at him once, from this angle. The quality of his gaze had shifted—as if he were not admiring my physique but trying to enter it, to suck up everything I knew, hold every thought in his hands. The quality of his attention disturbed me—but I focused on the fact of it, which surrounded me in a light not as pure as the sun, maybe, but like one of those heat lamps.

He was holding an empty water glass. He pressed the glass upside down over the deck like in the game where you ask a question and wait for the ghost to jerk the cup across the table—left for yes, right for no. If he let go of the glass, it would coast straight into the toe rail.

Smell this, he called.

And I saw there was an insect in the glass—a cockroach or palmetto bug.

I rolled off my bench and joined him on deck. He lifted the cup. The insect released a rank odour like rotten fruit. And it looked like rotten fruit. An oily date with stubbled legs and TV antennae. Patrick set down a sugar cube. He steadied the roach and the sugar cube with his spare finger.

I like cockroaches because they're armoured, he said. Something glinted in his hand. He was holding a straight razor. —See this? he said. This is the thorax.

He lifted the straight razor to my sternum. —It's this part. From now on I am going to call my own chest a thorax.

The blade pressed against my skin as he laughed. —I guess it's not the same for women. His eyes caught on my chest as he lowered his attention back to the insect, who was exploring the sugar cube with its antennae. —Here they have holes for breathing, he said, swiping the air next to the roach with his blade, indicating the underside of its abdomen. —Isn't that neat?

The blade made a wet crunching sound when he sliced the insect in half. There were now two sides, each with its own antenna, which twitched as the final pulses exited the body.

Gross, said Patrick. He crumpled his nose. —I'll call this one Castor, he said, pointing his blade to one half of the insect. He flicked the blade to the other half. —This one's Pollux.

I didn't say anything. I went into the head to wash my hands.

The Islas Coronados were four islands fifteen miles south of San Diego. We anchored at the southern island, in a slender cove. In the twenties and thirties, smugglers had used the islands to run booze into California. There was even a casino. Aside from the wind-scraped foundations of the casino, which had closed when the Mexican government cracked down on gambling, you wouldn't find a trace of humans now, but several species of cactus, petrels, snakes, lizards, sea mammals, feral cats.

For dinner, Joan fried banana fritters and Spam. I tried not to think of the insect as I helped her cook. I tried not to see bristled legs in the bananas, which I also sliced lengthwise. Joan tapped the spotted pink mass from its tin. I tried not to look at it either. Every now and then, she opened the wrong cupboard or paused over the stove as though she had forgotten what she was doing. Her hands remained still, or folded in her green embroidered apron. I watched from my corner of the counter, where I now snapped the woody ends off asparagus. Eventually, I wiped my palms on my shorts and stepped toward her, rested my hand on her back.

Are you okay?

Yes.

She remembered what she searched for, salt, and sprinkled a pinch over the wedges of canned meat. Then she reached for the halved bananas, which I had fanned over the plate in a sunburst. She dunked each crescent in the batter and tossed it in the pan.

We ate in the cockpit. The sun's disc plunged nearer to us, sinking behind the island. As we'd approached this cove, the sunset narrowed the sea somehow, erecting a wall along the westward ocean that we followed between North Coronado, which looked like a pregnant mermaid floating on her back, and the middle islands. One of the middle islands was called Pilón de Azúcar, or "pile of sugar," which I liked.

We ate without a table, Joan opposite Kenneth, Patrick opposite me, paper plates balanced on our laps.

Would you look at that sky, said Kenneth.

The light was a sulphurous orange.

Joan shrugged, sipped her milk.

One of these days, said Patrick, we'll sit here admiring the sunset, as we're doing now, and it will turn out to be the reds nuking us from Moscow.

Oh come off it, said Kenneth.

I'm telling you, said Patrick. He nodded to his left. —If that's not the colour of nuclear armageddon, I don't know what is. Do you know how many civilians died from napalm in Tokyo? No one talks about that, he said.

Kenneth clunked his beer bottle down beside his foot. —Napalm's not a nuclear weapon. It's chemical.

What about Hiroshima and Nagasaki? I ventured, looking at Patrick.

People talk about them, he said.

Joan glanced at me with impatience. I didn't know what I'd done wrong and looked back at her.

It wasn't the most sheltered anchorage and every now and then a swell rose and rocked us. I fixed my gaze on my plate and sliced the food into smaller morsels. I think the others were feeling queasy too, because our conversation quieted into this rhythm of focused chewing as the water lifted us and let us drop. Then Joan broke the silence.

You're eating loudly.

She laid her bare foot on Kenneth's shoe.

He tightened his grip on his fork. He opened his mouth and brandished a tongue lumped with masticated Spam and asparagus. —What did you say, dear? I didn't hear you, he said, clashing his teeth together.

A trace of smile played on her lips, and I thought, So this is how their marriage works.

Across from me, Patrick sawed his Spam, inserted a morsel and chewed for a long time. I found myself imitating him—grinding the food more than normal to match his pace. Perhaps he noticed, I don't know, but his gaze lingered on me again. He still watched me with a fullness I hadn't encountered from other boys—as if he hoped to memorize the bone of my collar, the shape of my ears, the gap of fabric under my armpits. I felt compelling. Even the way I sipped my milk was important.

We played canasta until we couldn't see without lighting the lamps. Then Joan excused herself to bed. I followed. The galley sink offered more room to wash than the heads, so we brushed our teeth there side by side. We spat, rinsed our mouths, and as I reached for the towel to dry my chin, Joan gripped my wrists with both hands.

I'm glad you're here, she said. Thank you for coming.

I laughed, embarrassed. —Sure. I wanted to come.

She drew me into a hug, her arms locking rigidly around my shoulders so I had trouble breathing. —You're a good sister, she said.

I couldn't relax in her grip, so I remained poised that way, folded under her chin until she let me go.

Her expressiveness bothered me as I climbed into my berth. Did she know something I didn't? Had she heard from Mom? After the wedding, the remains of our mother-daughter relationship deteriorated. I used to marvel at her composure, the beauty I felt certain she possessed. I imitated it. That was the only way to love her—in imitation. But in school I met other women her age, teachers who embraced me with warmth.

Not strategically like she did, but physically, emotionally, with all of themselves behind it. For them it was instinctive. When I realized that warmth, even love, could be instinctive, not a decision that shifted from one day to the next, based on mood or motivations, I didn't want to be like Mom anymore. Yet I feared that if Eugene or I left, she would perish. And Eugene could take off any week now. Frankly, I wouldn't have blamed him if he did.

Part of me wondered if Mom could live with them in San Diego. They had that house, after all. Then I could leave Victoria. For what, I didn't know, but all my dreams were predicated on going. To Vancouver, maybe. Or Europe. These thoughts lingered with me as I drifted off—the Sorbonne inviting me to study. My French wasn't great yet, but that didn't matter in my fantasy. I would meet a patient Frenchman who, as I sunk deeper into sleep, resembled Patrick. So I woke with a start when my door opened and I found someone at the foot of my bunk.

I gasped, scooted up the mattress into a sitting position. When I saw it was him, my breath calmed, but I continued to clutch the sheets around my chest.

I can't sleep in my berth, he said.

I continued to stare. He wore nothing but an undershirt and briefs.

So? I said—trying to sound harsh, though I felt myself softening toward him, as if he were my brother awake from a nightmare or wetting his bed.

Can I sleep with you?

I knew I should say no. But I didn't want to hurt his feelings.

There's no room.

We can make room.

I slanted my eyes at him—signalled with a frown that I would allow it but considered the request inappropriate.

He climbed onto the mattress. I pressed against the hull to leave as much space behind me as possible. He, in turn, crimped around my body. He left a polite gap between our hips, but folded his arm over my waist and lay his cheek on my pillow. His feet and knees slotted behind mine, the skin of his toes clammy, making me shiver.

Try anything and you're dead, I said.

His nose brushed against my neck as he nodded. For the second time that day, his breath tickled my ear.

15

He slipped out of the bunk at dawn and returned to his cabin. He had kept his word—he touched me as much as he needed not to fall off the bunk, no more. I decided not to bring it up. Events between him and me seemed to occur on another membrane, which pulsed, here and there, into the membrane we all occupied, but which contracted when a third person entered the room. I remembered our interactions as I remembered dreams, with doubt, and if I mentioned that night to him, I expected him to look at me questioningly. I didn't trust that my subconscious hadn't invented the whole thing.

In the galley, Joan crushed an orange with a palm-held juicer. Kenneth slumped on the settee, a day-old newspaper spread between his hands. The air smelled sweet, of maple and hickory from the bacon, which Joan slid onto a paper towel. She was toasting bread in the oven, in a wire rack over the gas flame. When the bread had darkened, she bent in time to remove the rack and set it on the stove. Her competence still marvelled me—when forced to cook in the past, she had improvised terrible concoctions, once adding pickled beets to spaghetti because she ran out of olives. Maybe her mother-in-law had stepped in, demonstrated a few recipes. Or she taught herself from magazines. The sea was tranquil compared to the day before, but Joan stood with a wide stance, as if braced for the yacht to lift and drop any moment. Still, her hands moved gracefully, like she had rehearsed where to step when the yacht dipped, the orange and the juicer in one palm while she flipped the bacon with her other hand.

Morning, she said.

Good morning.

I sat opposite Kenneth and tried to read the back of his newspaper. A headline about Kuwait's independence caught my eye, but he flattened the paper onto the table before I could read. Then Joan did something odd. She left the bacon on the towel and sat beside me.

Could you pass the editorials? she asked.

Kenneth leaned back. The top buttons of his shirt were undone. I couldn't see any chest hair. He slid the paper across the table. —It's a day old.

Oh really, said Joan. The *Union* doesn't deliver here?

He paused, arm still stretched from passing the paper across the table. A nerve in his lip beat. He retracted his arm and lowered his eyes to the section of paper he had kept for himself.

Is Patrick on deck? I asked, to remind them of my presence.

Yes, said Joan. She answered so quick I knew she hadn't read a word of the paper. She trained her eyes on the page nonetheless.

Won't the bacon get cold? said Kenneth.

Mm, she said. I'll have two pieces.

Kenneth sighed, exchanged a look with me, as if I must be used to her moods. It's true, she and Mom used to work themselves into athletic screaming matches. But her tone was different now.

I'll get the bacon, I offered, though I sat in the centre of the settee, boomerang in shape. One of them would have to stand to let me out.

Allow me, said Kenneth. He shifted off the bench, snatched the toast rack from the stove, the plate of bacon. I climbed after him to fetch the orange juice Joan had squeezed, which she had placed on the galley stove for balance.

Have you already had coffee? I asked.

Yes, said Joan.

I twisted the top chamber from the moka pot and dumped the grounds in the bag we had strung on the cupboard door for garbage.

You're in a queer state this morning, said Kenneth as he wedged back behind the table. —Did you sleep poorly?

She reached across the table for a strip of bacon and punctured it with her teeth.

Because if you're sleeping poorly, said Kenneth, you may as well take my watch tonight.

I slept fine.

If you say so.

Patrick, do you want coffee? I called toward the companionway.

Joan, said Kenneth. You're indecent.

Her bathrobe had parted. A breast slouched between two thin panels of fabric. I looked away, scooped coffee from the tin into the metal filter. A spoonful of grounds trembled onto the floor and I knelt to wipe them with a dishcloth. When I rose, she still had not secured her robe. A crumb of bacon had fallen to her nipple. She pressed it with a finger and sucked the morsel back in her mouth. Kenneth's stare hung off her breast. Serenely, she fastened her robe and stood from the table. She reached in her pocket for her cigarettes and climbed the steps to the cockpit.

The air was so sluggish we decided to stay anchored for the morning until the wind picked up. Then on to Ensenada. Kenneth kept saying "It's no race," which made me think he really did want to go faster but felt constricted by his crew, which was essentially Patrick. And though he'd used the motor a few times, he wanted to avoid long distances because of the sound and the smell, and "if I'd wanted to motor, I'd have bought a motor boat." So we would enjoy the islands for now. After Ensenada, there would be nowhere to anchor until San Quintín, which wasn't much of an anchorage at all, he said—just a morsel of land you duck behind to stay out of the wind. It was unlikely we would make it to Cedros Island, which we had talked about, but Kenneth wanted to avoid crossing Sebastián Vizcaíno Bay anyway. The Pacific rollers could be huge this time of year.

After breakfast, I tucked an avocado into my shirt pocket and followed Joan into the cockpit. Everyone had treated her marriage as a triumph. Our schoolteachers, the neighbours, even our mother bathed Joan in approval. Their congratulations on my As thinned at the same time, as if school achievement was a childish distraction of mine, with no bearing on the real world. Perhaps they were right, but I didn't know how else to be. Every now and then a clot of destructiveness inspired me to smoke cigarettes with friends and kiss boys I did not like instead of preparing for exams—but ultimately I woke in the night, rattled with nerves, and read my notes so furiously, I completed my exams with vigorous if shaky handwriting, and the teachers complimented my "fervour." But I envied Joan this bath of approval. As if she had done her bit now. She had married; she was no longer a burden to Mom or Eugene.

Patrick sat on the foredeck with a book in his hand. I made sure not to look at him as I climbed from the companionway. The fog was still lifting, and the air remained cool, but Joan had not added a layer beneath her robe. She had tightened the sash around her waist and hiked up her socks, which must have belonged to Kenneth—mustard yellow, pouching at the heel.

I brought you an avocado, I said, sitting beside her on the bench.

She glanced from her magazine. —You didn't have to.

I halved the avocado with a butter knife. —What are you reading?

Horoscope.

Can I see?

I passed her half the fruit and a spoon. She traded me the magazine.

Read mine, she said.

I flattened the centrefold on my lap and scanned the page for Taurus. —A better week to meditate than to act. A certain amount of hindrance is around, and you should make plans carefully. Saturday is your brightest day. Especially for moving about.

Her eyes shifted to the water, which barely lapped against the hull. —Ironic enough, she said. What's yours?

I carved a petal of avocado with the butter knife and smeared it to the roof of my mouth. —A tendency toward family misunderstandings and upsets could mar this week. Avoid arguments and extravagance. Try not to offend.

She laughed. —Good thing you're the least offensive person I know.

I had balanced another rift of avocado on my knife, but the hard edge of her voice made me lower it, scrape the flesh back into the husk.

What do you mean?

Nothing.

I lay the knife on the magazine, not caring that it left an oily smudge.

What? she said.

Nothing.

You're annoyed.

No I'm not.

The fog had lifted enough now that my bench pointed into the sun. I tossed the magazine to one side and pushed the sunglasses from my hair to the bridge of my nose.

You're unfair to Kenneth, I said.

Her eyes scanned my sunglasses a moment, then lowered to the avocado, which she hadn't touched. I watched with guilty satisfaction as her fingers tightened around the spoon. She scored the green flesh and lifted a portion to her mouth.

That's none of your business, she said.

I'm just observing. You know, as a third party. He's very patient with you.

Patrick could hear every word if he wanted to. But he appeared distracted and I didn't care anyway.

You're sarcastic to him, I continued, Mom's voice filling my head. —Belittling, I said.

At least someone around here says what she thinks.

What's that supposed to mean?

She tilted her cheek toward her shoulder. The sun glinted off her earring. —You only say what pleases people.

That's not true.

She nestled back against the cockpit coaming, as if to get a better look at me. Then she said her cruellest thing. —You're turning into her, you know. You don't see the glass as half-empty or half-full. You see a glass, and you fill it with whatever's in front of you.

In that comment, she confirmed all my fears: I was an empty glass. A mirror. My existence depended on who looked back.

That afternoon, Patrick and Kenneth optimistically weighed anchor. We made some progress south, but the breeze died again after a few hours, and Kenneth decided to lower the sails until the wind picked up.

Patrick dozed on the aft deck, the soles of his feet together, knees splayed apart. I thought he might adjust his position when I sat next to him, but no. I opened my copy of *The Old Man and the Sea*. Patrick saluted two fingers at me and shut his eyes.

In front of us, Kenneth hunched at the helm. He teetered on one leg, his right foot hoisted onto the wheel so he could clip his toenails. On the other side of the yacht, Joan smoked cigarettes and ashed them into the crease of her magazine. It's miserable to fight with someone on a boat—you can't get away from them. Below deck, the heat was intolerable, and you knew they were above you anyway, you could hear their footsteps. They were always, always within earshot.

Patrick's chest barely expanded as he breathed. That's how I knew he wasn't sleeping. His eyeballs hummed beneath his lids. He would be able to smell the lavender oil I had stolen from my sister's suitcase and wiped along the bones of my collar. It helped her sleep.

I couldn't focus on Hemingway. The fictional sea layered over the real sea made me feel queasy. The view of land had receded over the last few hours, though we continued to follow the scabrous outline of its shore.

What are you reading? Patrick said then.

I rotated the book so he could see the jacket. He didn't open his eyes. He slanted in the chair, heels shined out, one side of his unbuttoned shirt wedged under his armpit. His face had retained the feminine angles from childhood—the lift of his cheekbones, blond eyebrows tidier than my own, floral lips.

What's it about?

If he opened his eyes, he would see a sinuous man slumped in a skiff on a yellow sea.

A fisherman, I said.

He rocked his skull along the wood slats to find a comfortable gap to rest in.

Will you read it to me? he asked.

The book?

Sure.

Why?

His tongue darted over his lips. The sun had parched them. I thought he might need a glass of water.

Should I start from the beginning? I asked.

No. Read where you are now.

So I opened the book to the page marked by my finger and licked my own lips.

The passage described the fisherman's dreams, which no longer featured storms or women or fish, but lions on the sand.

What do you dream of? Patrick asked, interrupting me.

I dreamed a lot, but right then I couldn't recall anything

recent. —I don't know, I said. Maybe I'd have dreamed last night if you didn't disturb me.

Didn't you sleep? He opened his eyes for the first time. His irises blued deeper as his pupils shrunk.

What do you dream of? I asked him.

I don't.

Come off it. Everyone dreams.

I don't, he repeated.

We sat in silence. I returned to the book. The old man was peeing now. He peed against his shack. Patrick's moods confused me. I wondered if we would talk again, or if this was it.

What books do you read? I tried.

What people tell me.

You mean recommendations?

No.

It disappointed me to see his desire contract. I assumed that's what this meant. Like any tension, his desire had stretched, released, zinged back the opposite way.

I read what teachers assign me, he said, after a long pause in which I had forgotten my question.

How imaginative, I said, though I read what people told me too. Every book I'd packed had been on a course list.

He smiled—recognizing this fact, or else amused by the cruel slant to my voice, which I had never taken with him before. I pushed it further.

Do you think what they tell you too?

Only the pretty ones.

That response irritated me most of all. I released a noise of exasperation and opened the book again, searching the words I kept abandoning mid-sentence.

A friend of mine at Cornell is from Ankara, he said. He tells me what to read. He's a poet.

I trained my eyes on the text, as if Patrick's anecdote uninterested me.

He's pretty?

He has excellent taste. He wanted to impress a girl, someone we both know, who writes plays. I helped him find the words to translate the poem of a Turkish writer he admires. A communist.

He dragged out the word "communist." I had a feeling he made that up.

You want to hear?

I guess.

It's a love poem.

He rolled on the deck to face me, his body bracketed into a fetal position, his cheek propped by his hand.

Loving you is like eating bread dipped in salt, / like waking feverish at night / and putting my mouth to the water faucet

It continued from there. When he finished reciting, I looked down. I studied a bruise that had formed above my kneecap the shape of a limpet shell. My pulse wobbled in my throat. He had not blushed when he said "loving you." Who was loving, I wondered. Who was "you"?

16

THAT EVENING THE OCEAN WAS a texture like mercury, which I half expected to fragment on the sides of the yacht. As if to emphasize our stagnation, Joan and I still hadn't spoken to each other. Partly as a peace offering, partly because Joan hadn't moved to, I started the meatloaf.

Our stillness amplified the volume of every movement on deck, as well as their bickering. On the first day, voices were licked into the wind and the creak of the masts. Now I could hear every word she and Kenneth said. I considered shutting the companionway hatch—paused for a moment, knife hovered over the onion. But her feet appeared on the steps. She leapt the rest of the distance, thudding onto the sole, and charged past me to her cabin. A moment later, Kenneth followed, looking wearily calm.

Fumes from the onion bit into my eyes. I set the knife down, leaned against the counter, waited for the blindness to pass.

I only asked if you were changing for dinner, said Kenneth. His voice sounded strained, as if he had repeated his point more than once.

You said I looked coarse.

I didn't mean it like that.

How else do you mean that?

Their voices silenced for a moment. Then Joan said, Do you have a request?

Don't be severe.

What sounded like my sister's foot slammed into the built-in closet. Hooks of metal hangers scraped across the rail.

Choose, she said. Do you like this one?

Joan.

No? Too much skin? How about this? You've said it features my breasts nicely.

I tried to shut them out. I lifted the knife again to slice onion. Their argument reminded me oddly of a photograph we had seen years ago in our mother's *Cosmopolitan*. An American girl marches down a sidewalk in Florence. Behind her, a man grinds into his scooter, one foot on the sidewalk, mouth open in laughter; another leans in his chair, elbow folded over the seatback; another bends and coos to her, hand pressed to his trousers; another watches her from the shadow of a pillar; another stands flat-footed, pelvis thrust out, jacket over his shoulders, mouth stilled mid-speech; fifteen men in total, eyes lurching after her. Even as girls we recognized that scene, though we'd never been to Italy.

A sound of thrashing emerged from their cabin. —How's this?

I couldn't bear it any longer. I wiped my hands on my apron and left the counter. But Kenneth had not shut the door, or the door had rebounded when he slammed it. I saw my sister on all fours, a chiffon negligee wedged over her shoulders, her back arched, buttocks combing the air. For a moment, I feared he might charge the berth and ram her against the hull. But he did not. He stepped past me over the pile of clothes.

Joan's eyes landed on me in the doorway. Her chest

expanded and contracted. I guided her to sit. She pulled her knees to her chest, then let them spill open cross-legged.

You okay? I said, slotting a blue housedress back into the cupboard.

She stared at the wall. Her arms stretched to drape each knee. I could see her underwear, which I recognized from home—a cotton set Mom had bought in a six-pack. At the sight of her underwear, which I also owned, the last shreds of anger from that afternoon softened.

Why don't we dress for dinner, I said. I've started the meatloaf. Which pants were you wearing?

I lifted her white capris from the floor and snapped them in the air to flatten the creases. Underneath, a silk blouse lay crumpled. —That's a nice top. Where'd you find it?

Her eyes focused and unfocused at the wall, as if she were trying not to blink.

It's very European. Is it from Paris?

She sat like an Eastern monk, the solemnity of her posture undermined by the sunny chiffon nightie that barely covered the crease of her thighs.

Do you think I'm indecent? she said.

Of course not. The roots of her hair were damp with sweat. I guided her forehead toward my stomach. —You're the most decent person I know, I said.

He thinks I am.

Shh.

I pinched the blouse off the floor without removing my hand from her ear, as if separation would return her panic. I made a show of admiring the blouse in my hand.

Why don't you put this on, Joanie?

Who wants kids with an indecent woman anyhow. The children would be indecent. It runs in the family.

Put this on. You're working yourself up again.

Sheila's children will be *highly* decent.

That's enough, Joan. Take off the nightie. Good. That's it. Now put this on.

Later, I couldn't stop thinking about the woman in Florence. I was ten years old, Joan thirteen when we found the photograph. She ripped the page from the magazine and pasted it in her diary, which I wasn't allowed to read. I told Mom. Mom smacked her cheek without taking off her rings. Joan had to buy a second copy from her own money. After two weeks, I took the new magazine into my room and cut the photograph with scissors and pasted it into my own diary.

We had both been that woman. It involved Kenneth and Patrick. It involved my swim costume. The beach. The service station in James Bay, where girls from Joan's high school had asked men to buy them cigarettes. I used to follow her there. The men had wives at home, perhaps daughters, but they watched us as they filled their tanks, their eyes following our movement across the parking lot. They checked our bodies for newness—hips that softened over summer, breasts packed into last year's bras. In return, the girls received entire packs of cigarettes still in their cellophane. I was younger than the others, but the men liked my legs. Their eyes darted from my ankles to my knees, as if measuring the length of them, how slowly they could peel the socks from my calves. I had recognized in their stare both shame and want. It had thrilled me.

By dinner, the tensions of that day, as the other tensions I noticed, began to contract. Joan gazed into the middle

distance, with long intervals between each blink. Kenneth
chatted with Patrick about plans—whether to turn around
once the wind picked up or sail through the night to Ensenada.

The meatloaf tasted bland to me. For Mom, Eugene and
Luke, I prepared meals you couldn't bungle, like chicken
thighs baked in cream of mushroom soup. Kenneth seemed
to like it. He ate with his mouth open so you could see the
brown meat on his tongue. By contrast, Patrick carved his
slice into minute fragments. The more I watched him, his
shirt buttoned, though misaligned, one half of his collar
higher than the other, the more certain I felt he hadn't aged.
I knew so little about him—how he found university, who
his friends were, if he had a girl in Ithaca—and he knew
nothing of my life. Yet I recognized something. A trace of
myself, which I had marked all those summers ago, as he had
marked me.

A drop of salad oil fell on my breastbone. Both Patrick and
I looked to it. I wiped it with my finger. We ate in silence. Or
they ate. I practised a theatre of eating—pushing the meat
this way with my fork. Slicing it. Dabbing it to my tongue.

Around us, the sun imprinted its belly into the sea, coating
the waves with purple light. No one mentioned the dolphins
anymore. I was taken by how serenely the creatures swam—
they had internalized the rhythm of the surf, their dorsal fins
cresting the moment the waves peaked, then sliding back
under. I adjusted my breath to match them. I inhaled as the
dolphins lifted over the waves and exhaled as they dipped,
inhaled as they lifted, exhaled as they dipped. I closed my eyes
and continued to sense our movement: my breath, the yacht,
the dolphins linked by one body.

———

The wind picked up after dinner. We decided to sail through the night to Ensenada, Patrick and Kenneth alternating three-hour shifts at the helm. The restored motion of the yacht assisted the air of détente on the boat, literally a detension, and I slept deeply. My dream recalled an incident I had not thought of in years—when I had stolen a jar of cream from Roy's dairy wagon. In the dream, I saw only the jar tucked in my blouse, cream rinsing the sides of the glass, tuned to the rhythm of my torso as I pedalled. Just that. The sway of cream in a jar. I woke from the timber creaking and made a half-conscious note to tell Patrick next time he asked. So it wasn't as startling, this time, when the door opened.

He stood once more in white underwear. Perhaps it was the moonlight, but he looked malnourished. Ridges of bone bulged from his forearms. An arrow indented the gap between his pectorals, his ribs whiskering under his armpits. His thighs were all sinew: bone, tendon, vein twisted into rope.

Go to bed, Patrick.

I was on watch. It's Kenneth's turn now but I can't sleep.

So you wake me up?

He smiled in his impish way and shut the door behind him. —I won't stay long. You're awake now anyway.

You can be a real pill, you know that?

He climbed onto the bunk, sat with his legs folded to one side. His eyes dropped to the strap of my nightgown. I tugged the wool blanket tighter around my chest.

I'd like to kiss you, he said. It would help me sleep.

Cut it out, Patrick.

Just once. Then I'll leave.

I wondered how much Kenneth could hear from the cockpit.

One kiss, he said with a gentle smile. Then I'll go back.

He raised his eyebrows in a playful way, like Luke did when he asked for ice cream money.

Just one? I said.

He nodded.

Then you'll go?

That's right.

I lifted my mouth, eyes focused on the wall above him.

Not there.

I didn't know what he meant. He seemed pleased at my confusion. Excited by it. He parted the blanket from my lap.

Every muscle tensed as he bowed forward. I didn't move. I wanted to tell him to stop, yet I didn't comprehend what was happening. Then I realized I couldn't shift my jaw. I tried to start there—a twitch to release my tongue, so I could ask him to cut it out. But the bones of my mouth had ossified. I could no longer see his face. His nose touched the cotton between my legs. He breathed deeply. I felt a rush of air where he exhaled. He kissed the crotch of my underwear. After a moment, he sat up and flattened my nightie over my knees.

See? he said. Just one. Now you kiss me.

That wasn't the deal, but my jaw remained locked. He guided my head forward so it hovered above his groin. He moaned, anticipating my touch, and opened his thighs. The scent of him drifted from his underwear, which was blotted with moisture. I kissed him once.

When I sat up, he was grinding his teeth, his fist clenched into the mattress.

We're almost done, he said.

What did he mean, almost. I hardly noticed his hand close over mine. He guided me out the door toward his cabin. I didn't protest. His bunk appeared untouched, the top sheet folded over the wool blanket. He opened his toiletry case and removed a bottle of antiseptic.

Wipe yourself off, he said.

Again, I didn't understand.

He lifted a pair of shorts discarded on the floor and removed his white handkerchief. He passed me the handkerchief along with the bottle. When I understood what he wanted me to do, and that he wasn't going to turn away, I lifted the hem of my nightgown. I folded it high enough on my thigh so I could push down my underwear. I spilled antiseptic onto the cotton, the cold liquid dripping between my fingers. I clenched my teeth to avoid crying and dabbed my vagina. The liquid stung and smelled of permanent marker. He watched a moment longer, then nodded. I screwed the cap on the bottle and yanked the underwear halfway up my thighs before he stopped me. He guided me to sit down on the bed. He knelt on the wood sole and peeled my underwear to my ankles. I could see his nail brush on the bedside table, along with a pair of clippers. He nuzzled my groin. I focused on the nail brush. The antiseptic irritated the flesh of my vagina. His tongue chafed. After two minutes, maybe three, he pulled away and removed two clothespins from the toiletry case. Clumsily, as if undressing a doll, he yanked the nightgown over my shoulders. I sat naked on his bed. He opened a clothespin and clamped it around the base of my nipple. The jaws of the peg were high enough on my breast that the pain wasn't sharp—more of an ache. He burrowed back inside my skirt and licked me. The flesh under the pin started to bruise.

Can I go now?

Relief gushed at the sound of my own voice. Something in my tone must have alarmed him, for he sat back on his heels and wiped his mouth.

You're not enjoying this?

No.

I'm sorry to hear that.

I removed the clothespins and tugged the nightgown back over my head. He didn't stop me. The cotton chafed my nipples. I walked back to my cabin and closed the door. There was no lock. In bed, I shut my eyes and felt the throb of my vagina. It seemed to me the pain matched the rhythm of the sea.

17

I lay in bed the next day until everyone left the galley. Then I made toast, coffee, and carried it back to my cabin. I reinserted myself in the sheets, slid my hand under my knees, my ankles, to tuck the blanket in the gaps. I had not realized I'd been crying. In the mirror on the cupboard door, a grey eel blinked back at me. Yet my emotion felt disconnected from sadness or anger. More of a reeling. The way you lurch when the yacht pitches over a Pacific roller. Again and again. A reeling.

Mom had taught me how to drain puffy eyelids. You close your eyes and tap your finger on the swollen flaps of skin. The word "tap." Like plugging two faucets into your eyes and twisting the handles.

Around noon, Joan checked on me. I jumped at her knock. Willa?

My toast remained on the nightstand without a plate. I had placed it on *Metamorphoses*. The bread had grown cold, the butter congealed in a tract down the middle. I took the book onto my lap.

Are you okay? What happened?

I worried, for a moment, that I had lost my speech again.
But in the mirror, I saw myself shrug and say, Nothing.

You've been crying.

Allergies.

Out here?

The girl in the mirror shrugged again.

Joan's stare lingered on me. Then she turned to the metal
sink, straightened the hand towel.

We've anchored at Todos Santos. I thought we could go
for a dip while Kenneth sleeps for a few hours.

Okay.

There's another boat here too—they said we could borrow
their snorkels. You want to come?

Okay.

You're sure you're all right?

I'll get my swimsuit on.

It felt like a girdle that morning, the stiff cotton around
my stomach, digging seams into my upper thighs. I hadn't
eaten much, yet I felt bloated, ashamed of the flesh the suit
pushed from my waist. A blue stamp marked my breast
where the flesh felt tender. Another woman would have
slapped him.

Greta was bobbing near a twenty-foot sailboat called *Mozart*.
The family included three children, the parents and a grandmother. Our schooner looked ancient next to their fibreglass
vessel, three times its size. Kenneth's voice drifted to me over
the deck, where I rubbed suntan lotion on my shoulders. He
was shouting to two sandy-haired boys from the gunwale.

—You don't believe we're pirates? Then I guess you're not interested in joining our crew.

They had lent us their snorkels and masks. From the corner of my eye I watched Patrick float on his back. The mask encircled his face, the tube bracketing his cheek, like he didn't realize he had to face the other way.

I dove in before he saw me, muscled a path in the opposite direction until I could hold my breath no longer. Then I surfaced, wiped the salt from my eyes, treaded water in a circle to note our distance. He floated face down near the other end of the schooner. On one side of us, the south island rose—much grander than the Coronados, though scraggy, with tufted grass and cactus and guano-pasted rocks. In the other direction, a blue haze. We were too far to see Ensenada.

A girl stood on the deck of the family's boat. She wore red thongs, her hair pinched into a braid. She leapt into the water chest first and beads of water surged from her heels. From where I floated, the colours shifted and lost their shape. The seat of her swimsuit looked like an armful of yellow daffodils. Slowly, she rose by the crown of her head. Her braid lifted from her shoulders and pricked the surface. She could hold her breath a long time. I counted the seconds. Forty. Forty-five. Finally, she gasped to the air. A ribbon of hair slicked her cheek. She stared at me as she caught her breath. It seemed I was watching myself. Her suit sagged from her tailbone as she scaled the swim ladder and clambered onto the deck. Then she raised her arms over her head and dove back in. I dipped under water and opened my eyes. The girl's body formed a pale crescent, her chest punched out, legs arced behind her. Though it appeared dark from deck, the water was so clear it hung between us the colour of oxidized copper. The skin of her face looked green.

Now I counted forty-five seconds. Fifty. She rose first and I followed. A woman on the deck of the sailboat called her name. Lydia.

I have to go, mouthed the girl, though we had not spoken to each other. She turned and swam to the woman, who crouched at the ladder in a pink swim costume and matching lipstick. She held a towel.

At the stern of the sailboat, the grandmother washed herself with a pitcher of water. She had rolled the suit down to her hips. Her stomach pillowed over the lining, her breasts hanging from her chest like milky turnips.

I paddled around the stern of their boat, far from the schooner. What would happen if they couldn't find me? If I sunk under water at the right moments, held my breath for fifty seconds, sixty? I would probably make it to sixty. How long could I float out here? With the dolphins and albacore tuna. It occurred to me I didn't know what tuna looked like. I only imagined the fish in cans.

If I floated on my back, would the tide carry me to shore? In books, islands are fertile paradises with coconuts clacking off trees and fish you can spear from the shore. But who says it's not a sandy pip in the sea with a few gourds of wild cucumber?

Joan called from the deck of the schooner.

Another option was: climb onto the family's sailboat and stow away in the head. How long would Joan ask Kenneth to wait for me? The girl would teach me how to French-braid my hair. Joan didn't know how to French-braid either. That's why she kept it short.

I closed my eyes and experienced the salt on my skin, wizening my cheeks where it dried in the sun, the ocean under my heels, bearing my weight. I thought about ablution, the touching of clean water, the oils of last night curling into the sea.

When Joan called a second time, I swam back. She had dried off already and changed into an oyster-grey pantsuit, her hair parted and locked in foam curlers.

I heaved myself onto deck from the ladder, sensing the weight of my body. Patrick watched from the cockpit as I swept my hair to one side without wringing it. The sea water made me feel heavier, my bathing suit sodden, the water pooling around my feet. For a moment, I felt truly that I belonged in the sea. I was an octopus—a waterlogged sac on land, but nimble in the ocean, my limbs flowering and contracting to propel me through water, as petals open and close on a poppy.

Joan passed me a towel. When I didn't take it from her, she rubbed the terrycloth on my shoulders herself, careful not to dampen her pantsuit.

What's the occasion? I asked her, not looking at him. His eyes combed my thighs, red and puckered from cold, the indents over my bum where the suit had pressed its edges and now twisted into the crack.

Well I thought we were going to Ensenada, but Kenneth doesn't want to clear customs until we use this treat he brought from the clinic. So we'll have dinner here instead. He's sleeping now.

I couldn't imagine what "treat" would come from a clinic and cause trouble at customs, unless he had packed gross quantities of painkillers.

And then what? I said.

We'll overnight here and see Ensenada tomorrow.

That wasn't good news. I missed the sensation of forward motion. The terrycloth was irritating my skin, and this physical discomfort was amplified by Patrick's stare, which dared me to look back at him. I tore the towel from my sister's hands, wound it around my chest and skulked below deck.

I climbed into my dirty houseboy pants without drying my legs and buttoned a flannel shirt over my chest. I looked shapeless, a beached cephalopod, the flannel billowing over my hips. I wiped the hair from my face, twisted the strands into a bun.

Then I was in Patrick's cabin, sifting through the sweaty undershirts he had dumped on the floor. His toiletry case hung on the cupboard door. I unhooked the bag and sat on his bunk. Inside, he kept his razor and pot of cream, two horsehair brushes. Here also was a metal comb, toothbrush, tube of paste. Two spaces in the toiletry kit were vacant: one for nail clippers, the other for the nail brush, which remained on the nightstand.

In monster stories, the hero steals something from the demon for her protection: a nail clipping, an eyelash. I read about one demon in the Philippines. His knees arc above his head when he sits, he lives atop balete trees, in bamboo and banana groves. To subdue him, you leap onto the creature's back with a rope and pluck three spines from his mane.

I couldn't find clothespins, but I stole the nail brush and hid it under the mattress of my berth.

―――

It had been Patrick's idea to borrow nitrous oxide from Kenneth's dental office. The canister mounted over us on the galley counter. It looked like a missile. Kenneth watched it from the settee, as if his gaze could prevent the can from tipping over the counter. He scrambled from his seat and lifted the can, set it on the settee. When he saw I wanted to sit down, he lifted the cylinder again and placed it on the floor, his palm dropping a sweat print onto the blue metal.

It was Patrick's idea, he said for the second time. —I could get fired.

Joan stroked his hairline and hovered her mouth behind his earlobe.

You're just nervous, she whispered, then stepped back behind the galley counter. —They'll never notice.

Water lapped against the hull, but without movement for so long that I felt more and more claustrophobic. Patrick leaned against the cushion on the other side of the settee. His stare pricked me with every sweep of his eyes, from my over-sized flannel shirt to the bun I had pinned at the crown of my head. He lit a cigarette.

Joan took in my outfit also, but she didn't say anything. She dumped hamburger meat into a glass bowl and massaged the mass with parsley.

Did you catch a chill from the swim? she asked. You look pale.

Headache.

Kenneth, why don't you fetch her some Tylenol.

It's okay. It'll pass.

Kenneth.

He turned from the can, slid his hands into his pockets and headed toward their cabin. —Where did you say it was?

My purse. Hanging on the door.

She wiped her cheek on her shoulder, both hands plugged in the bowl of raw meat.

Will, can you grind pepper for me?

I joined her at the bowl, ground pepper into the scarlet

mass, which again I couldn't look at closely. I focused on the cheap candlestick someone had planted in the centre of the table—a rococo mermaid heaving the wax stub on her back, engraved grapes spilling lavishly down the nickel column.

You like it? said Patrick. I took it from my mother's.

His lips whitened around his cigarette. He released a long chain of smoke through his smile.

Excuse me, I said. I set down the grinder and climbed the steps to the deck. Behind me, Kenneth shouldered into the galley from their cabin. He said something with a rigid voice. A silence followed. I walked faster to the bow.

When I reached the side, I leaned over the gunwale. A school of fish hung suspended in the water, the light glinting off their bodies before the fleet lifted and tilted into the tide. I could hear Joan and Kenneth fighting in the galley. I tried to block out the sound, inhaled the ocean's salt on my skin, the tang of seagull shit dried onto the deck. Slowly, larger shadows overtook the shadows of the helm. Then these dark-nesses—spilled by the masts, the boom—were overtaken by the largest shadow, of Earth turning away from the sun. I closed my eyes. The wind fingered the curl that had dropped from my braid, dangling down the nape of my neck.

When I returned below deck, something had happened. All three of them sat on the settee with plates and hamburgers, though no one had called me to dinner. Nor had they started eating, but when I perched beside Joan on the end of the settee, Kenneth lifted his hamburger in both hands, as if he had been waiting. There wasn't enough room for me on the bench, but no one shimmied over. I clenched my butt muscles to avoid slipping. Patrick watched me take my place, then lifted his hamburger too. My sister clasped her hands in her lap, the whites of her eyes yellowed from crying. Kenneth fidgeted with his fork, spinning the utensil tines-down on the table. Without taking a bite, Patrick set his burger back down and began to saw it in half with his knife. Joan jerked one hand free from her lap. She shook the bottle of ketchup upside down and set it next to my plate.

The first bite of my hamburger drew only a mouthful of bun, which dried my tongue and made it difficult to swallow. I reached for my glass of milk. That's when I noticed the bottle of Enovid on the galley counter. I glanced at Joan. She felt my eyes, I knew, and didn't look back.

We ate—my sister's hands trembling under the table, her vibrations absorbed by my thighs wedged against hers; Kenneth, who hadn't spoken since he found the contraceptives in her purse; Patrick, who cut his hamburger in sixths before eating and kept laying down his utensils to palm his hair.

When Kenneth stood to wrest himself from the settee, he muttered something I couldn't hear except the word "solipsistic." He said it meanly, but I'd always thought there was something of the sun in the word—*sol*, like the Spanish. *Solar.* In dictionaries, the word comes from *solus*, alone, but maybe they are not so different, the sun and solitude. Maybe they need each other.

When Kenneth had disappeared above deck, I helped Joan clear the dishes.

Are you okay? I leaned to her over my stack of plates.

She looked at Patrick first, who studied us from the table, then me, before taking the plates from my hands and setting them in the sink.

I don't know.

I passed her the dish detergent, meeting Patrick's eye for the first time all evening. *Scram*, I mouthed. I turned to Joan. —Talk to him. I'll do these.

She pressed her hands to the bottom of the sink. The suds marked her forearms as the basin filled with water.

Patrick went up on deck. Joan dipped the plates in the water without rinsing them. I didn't say anything. I wiped the crumbs and rifts of foam with a towel.

If he doesn't like it, he can find a new wife, see what I care, she said.

You should talk to him.

What do you know? You're so good at relationships?

Eventually, the yacht pushed into motion. From the window, I noticed we were retracing our path from the cove, around the easternmost point of the island. We were headed back north. Not anchoring overnight or stopping in Ensenada. Kenneth had turned us around.

Patrick administered the gas in red balloons that he pinched shut with his fingers and passed over the settee table like soap bubbles. My sister closed her mouth around the rubber and breathed in and out, the balloon expanding and contracting. Eventually, she bowed away, her eyelids fluttering for forty seconds, maybe sixty. When he passed me my balloon, I pinched it tight in my lap. I felt wounded. Joan would rather humour Patrick than tell me what had happened. But I couldn't stand being left behind. So I took the balloon in my mouth and inhaled the gas, which wicked the back of my throat. Then warmth filled my limbs and their voices bent in my ears, and for a moment I wondered if we always saw our breath in balloons, would we realize how precious it was. In what felt like hours later, though no more than a minute could have passed, I woke with a cobweb of saliva latched to my chin.

Next, Patrick presented a mask attached to a breathing tube, which he screwed onto the canister. Joan lay back on the settee and shut her eyes. He fixed the plastic to her nose. A loose smile played on her lips as the gas streamed up her nostrils for one minute, two. Longer than I could hold my breath.

We took turn as his patients. We lay on the wood sole and he strapped the plastic mask over our noses. The sun filled our heads; his words slow like he sucked a crust of bread. The tension released from my body. I didn't even mind when he touched my breast. After a few minutes, he removed the mask and carried it to Joan, fixed it over her nose, the strap indenting the flesh of her cheek, stretching the baby hairs above her ear. Her eyelids closed, and I saw an openness I had never found before—her forehead long, unbroken by the pots of her eyes, extending past her pale eyebrows and the bridge of her nose. Patrick adjusted the nozzle of his can and we both watched her nod, the smile parting her mouth. As he stepped toward her, his shoe tipped over his canvas satchel, which sat beside the canister on the floor. The contents spilled onto the floor. I made them out from the settee: a pouch of clothespins, a length of frayed rope, from the locker in the bow, I guessed, safety pins, the bottle of disinfectant. He inserted a finger under Joan's collar and traced the drop of her neckline. Then his hand settled on the crotch of her pantsuit. After another minute, he removed the mask and strapped it over his own nose. I waited for his head to tip back, then reached for his satchel. I tied the rope around his bare ankles; he wasn't wearing socks. I tied a constrictor knot, which Dad had taught me. His hands flapped to remove the mask from his mouth, and I pushed it back. I unbuttoned my flannel shirt and parted it over my chest so he would think it was a game. I removed his shoelaces. Every time he nudged the mask away and nodded awake, I flashed him. Sometimes I massaged my breasts and pressed them together to make cleavage. A bulge built in his trousers. I pushed him onto his side so I could get at his arms. I bound his wrists with the shoelaces. Joan touched her fingers to her temples. She watched my actions with confusion in her eyes, as if she might be dreaming. After I yanked the knot tight, Patrick flopped onto his spine. I readjusted the mask on his face; the gas funnelled into his nostrils. I wondered how long you were meant to go under for.

Joan ran her eyes along Patrick's body, which had contorted on the floor like someone pushed from a window.

You should find Kenneth, I said.

What are you doing?

I tried to recall the thoughts that led us here, but my memories had unhinged, billowing in my head like bright, teasing clown fish. I saw the rope in his satchel, the clothespins on my breast. Strands of jellyfish branding my wrist, the rowboat. Joan in a blouse too large for her bust, pushing Kenneth against the well at the beach house. My mother's foot in a nude stocking. Ko-Ko's origami frogs. The phosphorescence. Three bears at the zoo on hind legs, their paws shining out.

I know what I'm doing, I said, though I didn't. A giggle rose like bile in my throat, but I kept it down.

Even at twenty-three, she could slash her eyes like a nun, her thumbs worrying the pockets of her pantsuit, the heel of her pump drilling the floor.

Go find your husband, I said. While you still have one. We both know you will anyway, so stop wasting your time.

She scooped the curls off her shoulder, scraped her fingers along her scalp.

Fine. You're on your own.

She dropped her hair and gripped the step rail. She climbed to the hatch. I really felt it, then: alone.

Patrick remained a crimped husk on the floor. A flash of sweat cooled over my forehead—what if I'd given him a brain injury? Had he been inhaling for too long?

My hands clattered to remove the mask from his nose. I bracketed my wrists under his armpits and dragged him toward his cabin, before Joan or Kenneth returned below deck. His chin knocked my knees. Then his head lifted, his eyes opened and he released a panicked shout. I lost my grip and his shoulders slammed to the floor. He writhed for a moment before he realized his forearms were bound. This discovery stunned him. He lay dumbly for a moment and I lifted him again, slinging him into his cabin. He tried to curse at me, but his jaw had slacked from the gas. His voice came out mangled, like an orangutan's. Still, I removed the handkerchief from his trouser pocket and jammed it in his mouth. He continued to grunt with only his throat muscles.

I couldn't heave him onto the bunk by myself, so I tucked a pillow under his head and draped the wool blanket over his body. I closed his door and returned to my cabin.

18

I decided to check on him. Joan had been outside for over an hour—if they'd heard us from deck, they ignored it. Patrick had stopped groaning, but I couldn't sleep. They could return below deck and find him. Or he could appear in my cabin with the straight razor. I pulled a flannel shirt over my shoulders and climbed from my bed. The yacht was pitched slightly to the side, and I had to drag my hand along the hull for balance. No sounds emerged from behind his door. I nudged it as noiselessly as I could, opening it enough to drop a splinter of lamplight on the floor. His eyes were closed, his breathing regular. I edged inside and stood in the corner, one hand against the wardrobe to brace myself. He lay slumped on his shoulder, wrists bound behind him, knees bent to his hips. I don't know how long I watched him. My perception of time felt unreliable; the seconds peeled with a languorous weight.

He had a funny look to him—like a fallen statue. Perhaps it was his pink lips, the curl of hair around his ear, his even tan, as if he were carved from expensive metal, the laces around his wrists—as in revolutions, when protestors topple statues with heavy rope. I wanted to touch him.

It started with his calf. He had a lean calf and it was easy to kneel beside him and rest my hand on his leg above the rope. I pushed my hand up his shin to feel his hair. I let my palm weigh on his kneecap, which looked so vulnerable then, you could feel every pit of bone. I slid my hand further up his thigh and let it rest on the warm bulge between his legs. A thrill uncurled in my belly. I lingered my hand on his crotch, and felt the muscle fill the nook of my palm. His eyes flashed open. I whipped my arm away and scrambled to leave. He fixed his eyes on his groin, as if he still felt the warmth of my hand.

He tried to say something like "wait," but the word was muffled by the handkerchief.

I hovered at the door. We stared at each other. He didn't appear scared. He knew I would turn back to him and remove the cloth from his mouth. I did so. The cotton was slick with saliva.

I have to pee, he said.

Was he lying? I couldn't let him go alone in the head. What if he severed the binds with the razor, or locked himself in and shouted for Kenneth? But he couldn't pee *here*. On the floor.

I'll bring you a bottle, I said.

Okay.

I found an empty pickle jar in the galley. When I re-entered the room, he had heaved himself into a seated position against the bunk. I closed the door behind me and switched on the bedside lamp. It surprised me he did not protest the binds, and I worried for a moment that he was enjoying himself—that this had been his plan all along. But when I presented the jar and said, A pickling jar for your pickle, he flinched.

I'm joking, I said.

I knelt on the rug and unbuttoned his trousers. I could not stop glancing at his face to be certain he had not rammed a paperweight in his jaw with the intention of plunging it into my skull. He shut his eyes. I lowered the zipper and opened a gap in his trousers and unbuttoned his underpants and lured the penis through the hole. Whatever hardness I'd stirred a minute ago had waned. It looked to me like a hairless rodent, too meek to venture into my hand. I lifted the jar higher. His eyelids tremored, the tendons in his neck clenched into thick lines, his entire body propped by its scaffolding.

Are you scared?

He didn't answer. It occurred to me, for the first time, "scared" was an anagram of "sacred."

After a long pause, he started to pee. The urine fell in spurts, then one ragged stream, the jar warming between my palms, filling with brass liquid. When he finished, I let him drip a few more seconds, then folded his penis back inside his underwear as quickly as I could. A drop of urine blotted through the cotton. I zipped his fly and wiped my hand on the rug, which had once been a rich thistle blue but was now coated with lint and dandruff.

Patrick slanted over his lap, his eyes fixed ahead on the door. Again, I was struck by how he did not struggle, or ask how long I would keep him here. Maybe he knew he could overpower me if he wanted, by shoving me against the wall or clamping his jaw on my neck. I visualized both scenarios as I sealed the jar of pee and pushed it under the built-in desk.

Do you want a glass of milk? I asked.

His hairless chin and moist eyes, the shine of saliva on his lip: he looked like a child.

Okay, he said. Could you fetch my bag at the same time?

So I returned to the galley. His satchel still lay on its side on the floor. I pushed its items back into the main pocket and set it on the galley counter. It started to slide back toward me.

I snatched it with irritation, slung it over my shoulder. I poured water for myself and a glass of reconstituted milk from the jar in the cooler. I listened for Joan and Kenneth's voices, but no sound seeped from the deck planks. They had stopped talking.

Back in Patrick's cabin, I crouched before him and lifted the milk to his mouth. He pulled too deep a sip and coughed, the liquid spattering my chest, dribbling between the buttons of my shirt. I dabbed the flannel with my hand. He watched. I shifted away from him to wipe the rest off.

Sorry, he said. Will it stain?

No.

I set the glass on the nightstand, which had a lip so it wouldn't slide off. He hadn't finished yet. When I turned back to him, he had folded over his lap, his arms stretched behind him.

Do you like this? I asked him.

Not particularly, he said, his head between his knees. Do you?

I'll untie you in the morning.

Why not now?

I don't trust you.

He nodded, a funny gesture upside down—his shoulders butting his knee tendons, his earlobes folding against his calves.

You may as well sleep, I said. Time will pass faster.

You could help. He lifted his head from his knees and straightened his back.

How.

He opened his thighs and bobbed his head forward and back, his mouth yawned open.

I hurled the wet handkerchief at him. —You brute.

In my bag you'll find a bottle of sleeping pills. I'll take a few if you want.

Why?

So time passes faster. As you said.

I found the bottle at the bottom, below the pouch of clothes-pins. The label read "Barbital," which Mom took at night too. I emptied three tablets into my hand and held it out to him. He licked them off my palm and I tipped the milk into his mouth. This time he pretended to cough, but the milk remained in his mouth.

Is that glass half-empty or half-full? he asked, once he'd swallowed.

The sweat cooled behind my ears, on the bone of my neck.

So you *were* listening.

Hard not to. He winked and slumped onto his side.

I biffed the back of his head. —Hey. I know those pills don't work that fast.

But he only smiled and rocked his cheek to rest on the rug. He lay there in silence, his eyes closed, for another few minutes.

I clenched a tuft of his hair and lifted his head. But I had nothing to say so I let go. The weight of his shoulder tipped him onto his chest. I knew he was pretending. I sat, convinced he'd lurch up and pull a face, for many minutes. By then, his sighs had deepened. I worried his torso would cut circulation to his hands, or that blood would pool in his head and clot.

I drank a sip of milk, which helped me think. We were sailing at a clip now, the vessel heeled to the right, so the whole room was slanted. I had to crouch and press my knee into the berth for balance. His hair was beginning to loosen from its bond of salt water. A strand of it fell toward his eyelashes, which were so pale they vanished into his skin. I knelt beside him on the rug and unpicked the knot. When his arms were free, I eased him onto his back and rubbed his wrists to encourage the blood flow. He was really asleep now, his snores scraping the roof of his mouth. I drank another sip of milk. It was strange to see him so harmless, like a bee with the stinger plucked. Midnight had passed, but I didn't feel tired. I could see into the satchel on the floor, and once again scanned the contents. It was a Boy Scouts satchel, the eagle and fleur-de-lis faded on the canvas flap. Inside, a pocket was labelled, in permanent marker, *Emergency sewing* and another, *First aid.* I removed the pouch of clothespins and withdrew one. Of course they were the same pegs he had used on me— wood, a metal coil. I had never realized how sinister clothes-pins looked—finger-sized mousetraps. I squeezed one in my hand, pressing and releasing the prongs like a beak. Then I closed the beak on Patrick's thumb. I waited, but he didn't stir. He breathed through his mouth, his snore starting to irritate me now. I fastened a peg on his index finger. I still had the blue pock where he'd clamped the peg around my nipple. A sweat released over my arms. Before long, I had pegged every one of his fingers and the webs of his thumbs. With every pin, I felt a pang of glee. Twenty pegs remained in the bag. I rolled up his shirt. I pinched what fat I could find on his flank and clamped it. Something extra sparked when I pegged his navel—the pleasure of slotting a book into its space on the shelf, or a teacup onto its saucer—as if the whole world were built from these tiny absences that invoked the presence of something else. I realized, as I pegged the lip of skin under his navel, where a trail of hairs climbed from his underwear, that I felt aroused. I unbuttoned his trousers and unzipped his fly and pulled down his underwear. His penis hung over his testicles like a toy-sized trunk. I re-exam-ined his body on the floor, his fingers and loose skin pinched with clothespins. I clamped another around the saggy skin of his scrotum. He stirred then. His head turned from one cheek to the other, and his brow tensed. My hand hovered over the peg. I released it and clamped the skin of his thigh instead. Then I clamped his butt cheek. When he didn't move, I tried another peg nearer to his anus, webbed with wisps of hair. Six pegs remained and I used four on his butt and thighs and one behind each knee. After, I sat against the wardrobe and observed my work. I felt a rush of disgust and couldn't tell whether I hated him or myself—as if we were those twinned objects, the absence of one programmed into the other. To silence my thoughts, I lifted my nightgown and slid my hand inside my underwear. I agitated my fingers back and forth and clenched my buttocks and came quickly, biting my free arm to silence each wave of pleasure. Then my hand deflated and I sunk back against the wardrobe door—eyeing him in case I had been too loud. When he still didn't show signs of waking I pulled myself up and shuffled to the metal sink and washed my hands. I returned to find his penis had swollen— as though he had recognized my quick breath in his sleep. I felt such shame, I couldn't look at his face as I removed the pegs. I buckled his trousers and returned to my cabin.

I woke from the sound, not the impact. *Greta's* planks were screeching, a high-pitched wail like humpbacks, as if we had intercepted a pod and they were nosing into the sides of the boat, vibrating their larynges. But the groans were accompanied by a harder sound—wood splintering, popping. I rushed to my porthole and couldn't see anything. For a moment I didn't know if the blackness was sky or water. Then a frothy wave lashed the glass. The sounds grew ear-splitting as I pressed my nose against the window. But it wasn't the cracks and pops that alarmed me. I realized, with sweat prickling my forehead, that I could hear metal. Steel cables ringing against an aluminum mast, though our masts were cedar. I recognized the clanking from the marina, the tension of cables working against wind, though what I heard now was arrhythmic—a clamour. It took someone shouting outside, Joan or Kenneth, I couldn't tell, to confirm something terrible was happening.

In a panic, I remembered Patrick. I shoved past the person who shouted, not taking in their face, only recognizing a darkness, a body blocking my path, and skidded into Patrick's cabin. The boat was pitched to one side and I nearly toppled over him onto his bunk. He was beginning to stir, though I noticed the roar was softer amidships. I tried to unpick the rope around his ankles, but I had tied it too tight. My hands rattled. Finally, I loosened the knot with my teeth and pried the rope over his heels, scraping his skin. He started to flail as I tugged him out the door. In the galley, Kenneth was helping Joan up the companionway steps. Then he reached for my hand. I let him nudge me into the wet air. Once outside, I turned and extended my arm to Patrick, who was having trouble finding his feet. He took my hand at the same time Kenneth pushed him from behind. Between the two of us, we lifted him into the cockpit.

Then all four of us stuttered to a halt. *Greta* advanced slowly, but steadily, through a fishing boat. The boat had parted in two—three passengers clambering onto the stern, which stayed afloat as the bow tipped nose first into the sea, the painted name, *Bagheera*, sinking as I read the letters and pronounced them in my mouth.

Kenneth shouted at Patrick to radio the coast guard. Then he rushed to the side of the boat and tossed a life preserver to the passengers. Joan helped him heave up the line. The first person who emerged was a boy, maybe fourteen years old, his cheeks chapped with cold, his hair dripping, eyes so wide with fear he could have been half that age. Without realizing what I was doing, I paddled him into a hug, clutched his body against mine until he stopped shaking. Joan, Patrick and Kenneth helped the remaining two on board. The last one, a Japanese man, struggled from their hands and shouted at the water. In this way, we learned that someone was missing. Kenneth shone what lights he could from the masts; Joan and I searched the galley for spare flashlights, lanterns. Then all seven of us shone beams into the waves, searching the debris for something that moved like a human, an arm batting the surf, a jaw opened for breath. We shouted his name, Erwin.

It was the boy who saw him, his blue shirt filled with sea and bloated like a sack. He wasn't responding to the preserver or our shouts. Then the Japanese man leapt into the water. He locked one arm under the man's armpits and reached for the preserver with his other, and together, Kenneth and Patrick tugged them on board. They tried to pummel the water from the man's stomach. Waves of it gushed from his mouth, but he didn't wake up.

2001

19

I BARELY RECOGNIZE THE CITY, aside from a few land-marks like Santa Fe Station. They've demolished many of the bungalows to carve space for high-rises. The glass reflects the sea on one side, hills on the other.

Joan had asked what I was thinking, to return here. I'd been unable to answer at the time. After seven days on the road with Mom, I began to understand why. Her question conceals a larger one: why now? Why have I waited?

There are a number of biographical facts I could list, start-ing with graduate school at McGill. McGill's Classics Department was the first environment I couldn't blend into. I was the only woman in my MA group. I felt, at times, like a stuffed peacock—eye-catching at first, until my colleagues forgot I was there. But the moment I spoke, their heads whipped to me. And I spoke a lot. To everyone's surprise, not least my own, I had opinions about the texts, about transla-tion, and I could articulate them. The professors didn't find me eye-catching; I worked harder to turn their heads. But I developed a friendship with an Ovid scholar from Montpellier. He supervised my MA and later, my PhD. If I posed a question in English, he responded in French, though he spoke English with his American students. We wrote letters and cards in Latin. It began when, in search of a book, he taped a note to my office door—*Ars Amatoria perdidi. Habesne est?* And I responded in kind.

I didn't leave Montreal until 1971, when York offered me my first teaching post. So if I return to the question of why I waited, one answer is work. *Keeping myself busy.* Which is another way of forgetting.

My sister lives more comfortably in the present than I do. It's a sticking point between us. She calls me the White Queen from *Through the Looking-Glass.* "Jam to-morrow and jam yesterday, but never jam to-day."

She and I forgot the accident by different modes: Joan in the present, through her divorce from Kenneth, her second marriage to a radio announcer in Vancouver. I in the future—never content with the city I'd landed in, moving from Montreal to Toronto, Vancouver, until full circle back to Victoria. We'd sold the home on Salt Spring Island by then.

I guess one aspect of aging is that the future grows limited. While Joan remained preoccupied in her ever-unfolding present—her divorce, her second marriage—I looked toward the past.

A few factors inspired me to go now, rather than five years ago, or next year—to eat jam today, for a change.

First, Mom turned eighty-five this March. Her dementia was taking over, but the doctors said she was in pretty good shape, physically—a surprise to anyone who knew her. One final trip, the two of us, seemed a nice idea.

Then, of course, there was the anniversary that passed. Forty years. I had recently installed cable internet at the house and found myself *searching*. I sent an email to the U.S. Coast Guard and asked for the investigation report. I called the San Diego County Medical Examiner, whose reports were accessible under the Freedom of Information Act. I learned that the *Union* archives were held at San Diego State University.

Then there was Patrick. It didn't surprise me that I had never seen him again. We lived in different parts of the continent. We were not a family that shared reunions, and after Joan divorced Kenneth and Mom left Eugene, nothing tied us. I knew from Joan that Patrick had married a woman from Cornell. They'd lived in Oceanside with their son and daughter. What's odd is: I couldn't shake the notion that a trance had lifted that night on the boat. Patrick's imprint on me, my imprint on him: they vanished. As if the moment our relationship pressed into someone else—even if cause and effect cannot be a hundred percent conclusive—our bond severed. For both of us. Neither one attempted to get in touch. Last month, Joan passed on the news that he had died. A gas leak in the house while his wife was on a cruise to Alaska.

20

THE LIBRARY ASSISTANT LOADED the microfilm reader for me. We had made the *Union*'s front page. The assistant didn't mention Mom, who sat beside me with her adult picture book, *Barn Animals*. Mom had just had her medication, which made her drowsy, and I could see she might nod off soon. She lay back in the leather chair I'd wheeled from an unoccupied reception desk. It had looked more comfortable than the plastic ones.

The headline read: *2 Vessels Crash; San Diegan Killed.* The photo showed a police officer covering Erwin Powell's body with a blanket. Behind them, I recognized the boy on deck. I couldn't remember his name. *In the background, Mrs. Walter consoles her son, 13, one of three survivors from the sunken boat.*

I turned the knob to the right to advance the film.

Cmdr. Geoffrey Banks, officer in charge of marine inspection, said persons aboard Greta *reported that there were no lights shining on the fishing boat when the accident occurred.*

Hayashi, however, told a reporter that the boat's mast light, which could be seen from 360 degrees, was on, and so was a light on the boat's bait tank at the stern.

The boy's name, I found out, was Sammy.

From the obituary, I learned that Erwin Powell had owned a bar called the Grotto for twenty years before he sold the property to buy the fishing boat with Haruto Hayashi. I have no idea what the link was between Powell and Hayashi. Nor the link between them and Sammy Walter. I don't recall much of that night, and none of the words spoken.

Mom began to snore in her chair—a nasal rasping that I tried to ignore. I felt conscious of students glancing in our direction.

The medical examiner's office mailed me a copy of their report a month ago. Some details have stayed with me. They help me know him.

The body was that of a well-developed, well-nourished Caucasian male of the apparent stated age, and was viewed lying on his back in a Stokes litter onboard the Mexican Coast Guard Cutter #95741 at the Coast Guard Landing, Shelter Island, San Diego, California. The body was cold, in primary rigor mortis, and was clad in undershorts and a nightshirt. The body was edentulous compensated. The hair was brownish gray. The eyes were hazel, pupils equal. Numerous abrasions and contusions of the thoracic region and of the left arm were noted.

I had to look up the phrase "edentulous compensated." It means he wore false teeth.

The body was identified by his brother:

Mr. Edward C. Powell, 1166 Barcelona Drive, San Diego, brother of the decedent, present, stated in substance that to his knowledge his brother (decedent) had no history of a heart condition. He stated further that his brother was a very strong swimmer and had participated in long-distance swims in the Great Lakes region and off the La Jolla shores. Mr. Powell stated further that the decedent was a bachelor.

I never located the coast guard report. When I phoned the National Archives, their search came up empty. The archivist said it was likely the record no longer existed, as accident reports were considered "temporary records." There were no follow-up articles in the *Union*, either. The media must have lost interest after that first week. I can only say what I know: Kenneth and Joan were on deck. I was in bed. Patrick's legs were bound in his cabin. Kenneth insisted he hadn't seen lights, but I don't know how alert he was, or distracted by his fight with Joan. Was Patrick meant to relieve him from watch? Would that have changed anything? The investigation proved inconclusive with regards to the lights. It was Hayashi's word against Kenneth's.

Mom was beginning to stir, so I rewound the slides, replaced the reel in its case and returned the case to the cabinet. I reminded Mom where we were before she got upset.

They make excellent Mexican food here, Mom. How about a burrito?

I suggested burritos because you could eat them with your fingers. Utensils were becoming harder for her to grip.

Grand, she said.

She linked her elbow around my arm, and we inched toward the front door. I couldn't get the newspaper image out of my head—his shape under a wool blanket.

He was unmarried. He swam the Great Lakes.

21

I'VE LEARNED TO ORDER A SIDE for myself, because Mom will only eat a quarter of her main. I nibbled on tortilla chips and guacamole while she attempted her burrito. She couldn't bite through the thick fold of tortilla, so I tore the whole thing open. She dabbed her finger in the paste of beans.

A young man sat next to us with a collapsible baby buggy. I would have called him a boy were it not for the buggy, the infant straddling his bicep. He ate a taco with one hand and jiggled the baby with the other. Black hair coated the baby's head. That's all I could see from my table.

The man sucked at his Coke through a straw. I could tell he was staring at me from the corner of his eye, to assess why I was looking at him, maybe. Yet I didn't want to look away. And I didn't want to say something grandmotherly, like, How old is he?

So I turned my tortilla chip in the guacamole until it was green and heavy and lifted it to my mouth.

He had a pack of cigarettes on the table, and I wanted one. The corners of his mouth were smeared with white sauce and I thought about wiping the sauce with my thumb—but that felt grandmotherly too. Then I thought about what I was wearing—my button-down denim skirt and an orange camisole, which I wore under shirts in the winter and as a shirt in the summer. I felt self-conscious. How would I look to him?

It's not that I wanted sex. He could have been my son—even my grandson. But I wanted him to look at me as a possibility, I guess.

Beside me, Mom pinched the rice with her fingers and spilled it down her chin when she chewed.

I smiled at the man.

He smiled back.

How old is he? I asked.

Six months.

He wore jeans and a white shirt. A tattoo of Jesus filled his right bicep, which I thought was a little on the nose.

I couldn't bum a cigarette, could I?

He lowered his taco and tossed the pack to me without disturbing the baby, whose cheek pressed against the tattoo.

Are you having one? I asked.

Nah, he said, nodding to the No Smoking sign in the window.

I'd already lit the cigarette and observed it now with some dismay as it burned at the end of my arm. I rubbed Mom's wrist, indicated I'd be back, and stepped outside onto the sidewalk. The sun beat onto my shoulders. Mom frowned at me through the glass. The man whispered to his baby. I smoked. I remembered how desperate she was for Roy's attention that summer.

Last year, Joan and I visited Mom for the first Thanksgiving of the millennium. We tried to make it festive, though Luke couldn't join us. Joan bought a bag of tissue-paper turkeys, the ones you find on bakery counters at Thrifty's. We planned to stay until Monday, when Joan would return to Vancouver to see her in-laws.

The first morning, I scooped coffee from a tin from the cupboard and two pearled maggots spilled out—clamping and unclamping till they burrowed back in the mound.

I gathered my senses. I tossed the grounds outside and resumed making breakfast. I had planned to surprise Mom and Joan with banana pancakes. When I located the jar where Mom kept her flour, I noticed tracks: a larva-sized tunnel down the side of the glass. I opened the jar and parted the flour with a spoon. I lost count after twenty.

They had infiltrated the oats too. A strange crumb coated the pralines—moth eggs. Six or seven larvae had hatched in the peanut butter. How long had Mom been eating that food? Either without spotting the larvae or too embarrassed to ask for help.

We went out for breakfast that morning. When we returned, Joan and I emptied the cupboards and bleached the shelves. We bought new groceries for Mom and made room for them in the fridge.

For Thanksgiving dinner, I made turkey breasts stuffed with sausage and chestnuts. I didn't have an appetite—I imagined larvae carving trails in my potatoes. Joan had arranged the crêpe-paper turkeys in a row across the tablecloth. They seemed to watch us, silently tabulating.

I must have been looking at them, because Joan asked if they were bothering me.

No, I said. I guess, do we need so many of them? I feel outnumbered.

She gave me one of those looks like, *Are you losing it too?*

———

The same evening, Mom's facial recognition started to go. At least, that was the first time we couldn't dismiss it. She sat at the kitchen table, folding and unfolding her napkin while we cleared dishes. I was about to lift the gravy boat when she tugged my sleeve.

Honey, she said. When are you going to drive that girl home?

What girl, Mom?

It took a moment before I realized she meant Joan, scraping kale salad into a container.

She can't take the school bus. It's nighttime.

That's Joan, Mom. She's sleeping here tonight.

Like hell she is.

I asked her GP and the nurse about travel. They thought she could manage if I took precautions. First, they recommended we drive—the Miata would be less stressful for Mom than airports or train stations. I carry a bag of essentials at all times, which includes: medication, health and allergy information, a clean change of clothes, water, snacks and activities. I gave Joan and Luke copies of our itinerary with phone numbers. In the glove compartment, I keep a file with doctors' names and numbers, a list of medications and dosages, addresses for local police and hospitals, emergency contacts, insurance information. In the back seat: her favourite jigsaw puzzle, a Discman, Anita O'Day and Patsy Cline CDs, beads, fishing line. She loves stringing beads.

We took a week—driving no more than five or six hours each day. We stopped often for peaches, cherries, ice cream. Every afternoon, we found a new motel, each with a green swimming pool and polyester bedspreads. At times, we drove with the top down, singing Patsy Cline. Mom grinned from the sun hat that tied under her chin as if we were on some great escape. At other times, she grew anxious. She wedged her hands under her bum and sat very still. Or she gripped her head to stop the wind from buffeting her ears. Then I would do up the top. I'd put a quiet CD on the Discman for her, or we would stop for a stretch. If she asked where we were, I said we were driving to California. Every time, she nodded as if that made all the sense.

It occurred to me as we drove that both Victoria and San Diego exist on a border, a southernmost tip: one nudging the forty-ninth parallel, the other a twenty-minute cab ride to Tijuana. They are mirror towns—each side resembles the other, but not quite; the images are flipped.

22

We're at a hotel near the Little Italy sign. We have a pleasant courtyard, where Mom and I string beads or put together her lighthouse puzzle. For breakfast, we order cappuccinos and *cornetti* from the café.

Today I write from the courtyard while Mom naps. I taped a sign to the phone with my cell number in case she wakes up, but I'll check on her when I finish my glass of wine.

A lot of boys could be Patrick, here. When I imagine how he used to be, I keep thinking of peanuts: a thin shell of armour. Sun-brown. Two faces that turn into four faces, both at each end. The Latin name for peanuts is *hypogaea*, or "under the earth."

Back in Victoria, I've been working on a translation of Ovid's *Fasti*. *The Book of Days*. I started the project in the new millennium, but the house repairs have kept me busy. So has Mom. Still, I've enjoyed tinkering with the odd passage on a Sunday morning, as you would a crossword puzzle. Ovid wrote the *Fasti* as a treatise on the Roman calendar, starting with the first day of January. The work we know ends in June, though the first six books of the poem allude to the full twelve months. One of his poems, addressed to Augustus, says he wrote the *Fasti* in twelve books, and though he planned to dedicate the entire work to the emperor, his exile interrupted him. It's not clear if that's true.

I completed January this spring. The month opens with a description of the poem's theme as a calendar. Then the speaker interviews Janus, god of passageways and beginnings, namesake for the month itself. His temple, Ianus Geminus, stood on the main road that approached the Forum from the northeast. No archaeological remains have been found, but its depiction on coins suggests a rectangular building with two arched doors. The long sides were constructed from ashlar blocks, which culminated in a frieze of vines and palmettes. One gate faced east, to greet the rising sun, the other west. The two directions represent the god's faces—one fixed on the future, the other fixed on the past.

Here's a passage I've translated from the middle of Book 1: *Kalends*.

> I've told you my name, now learn my shape
> though you already understand it in part.
> Every doorway has two sides, outward and in,
> one facing the public, the other the home.
> And like a doorway seated at your threshold,
> who watches incomers and outgoers,
> so I, doorkeeper of the divine hall,
> look east and west at the same time.
> You see Hecate's faces turned three ways
> to guard the forking crossroads:
> where I, lest I lose time swivelling my head,
> see both ways without moving.

This morning we ordered our *cornetti* to go and found Erwin Powell's house. I parked at a nearby supermarket and left Mom in the car with the radio on and her tin of beads. The bungalow sat at the far end of a road without sidewalks. It could have been built in the thirties or forties. Or more recently, I'm not sure. The cactus would have been there, though. It looked over a century old. Maybe the cactus connects us through time, if nothing else. Erwin on one side. Me on the other.

In the poem, the God of Doorways continues:

> Here, where Rome is now, uncut forests thrived,
> and all this was grass for scattered cattle.
> My citadel was the hill people of this age
> dubbed Janiculum after my name.
> I ruled then, when Earth could still bear the Gods,
> and deities mingled in mortal spaces.
> Justice had not yet fled the sin of mortals
> (she was the last god to leave the Earth).
> Honour, not fear, governed the people without
>   force,
> and it was no labour to expound the Right to
>   righteous men.
> I had nothing to do with war: I guarded peace
>   and doorways.
> And this, he said, exposing his key, was my weapon.

23

I'm told they have cameras strong enough to view individuals from airplanes. I always thought what you see is what you get with photographs—but really there's no limit to how close you can look. When a weaker camera takes a photo, the details simply fade as the contrast between light and dark reduces. In these images from airplanes, a grown human occupies one pixel. Imagine if you were to watch traffic: you could follow a white van the size of a Tic-Tac up the I-5 at the same time you trace another Tic-Tac along Imperial, our yellow Miata, for example, which turns left onto 28th as the white Tic-Tac exits onto 19th—and then perhaps a Mercedes turns onto Broadway, so if you imagine this aerial camera, taking photos every second with a high-resolution lens, all three of us travelling along different streets, the camera could track all our lines through space like stocks on a graph—one Tic-Tac veering onto a side street, another pulling into a drive-thru taco stand, then swerving together again until our paths converged. Two Tic-Tacs might drift side by side for years before their lines intersected.

I've had a few serious relationships, but to this day I felt most exalted with Patrick. Even that word, "exalt," from the Latin *exaltare:* the prefix *ex* means "out or upward"; *altus* means "high." Consider other words of the same root: "alto," "altitude," "altar," the platform used in worship. But it does humans no good to be worshipped.

Another word I think about is "spinster." From the Middle English *spinnen*, "to spin, a spinner of thread." Before the industrial age, spinning wool provided income for a woman living independent of a man. The modern usage of the word implies someone childless, fickle, prissy, *beyond the marriageable age*, repressed. After her separation from Eugene, Mom used this word. I would say, *Technically, you're still married to Dad*, then quote Elizabeth I: *If I follow the inclination of my nature, it is this: beggar-woman and single, far rather than queen and married*. She'd reply, *Easy for her to say*.

I like the word myself. I imagine a wooden top spinning precisely on its axis.

Yesterday I walked from the Gaslamp Quarter to the harbour, then all the way down India Street to one of the Italian delis. We have a kitchenette in our room, and I wanted to pick up ingredients for dinner: fresh ravioli, oil, oregano. I bought a slab of focaccia, which I ate on the walk back. I had worn my new sandals, because it was so warm, but blisters formed on the bottoms of my feet. I removed my shoes and continued on the pavement stones, mincing across a pebbly crosswalk. They say you only know a city if you walk it. I would like to add, if you walk in bare feet.

Then I saw him. Not as he looked last time, with the bowl of his pelvis showing, the twisted ropes of his thighs, and not as he looked in the obituary photo, his hair thinned, face marbled with sunspots, a hard shell of a belly under his golf shirt, but how I imagined him still—the most sublime version of himself, hair curled from salt, shoulders the sun could rest on. He looked thirty-one, thirty-two. He had the same swimming eyes and lips as if he'd been sucking on a cherry drop. A woman in a halter sundress held his hand. Patrick had raised his kids in Oceanside—it could have been his son. Or a total stranger. He wasn't the first man I'd projected his likeness onto. And yet.

I backed into a doorway and watched the man cross the street and open the door of a white BMW and watched the woman hand him her purse as she fixed the buckle on her shoe and watched them both get in and drive around the corner. And I saw all seven characters of their licence plate, and I knew I had time to write them down. But I didn't. A teenaged girl passed me through the doorway—I was standing, I realized, barefoot in front of a 7-Eleven. I stepped out of her way. I continued walking. I tore a piece of focaccia and crunched the salt between my teeth.

When I returned to the hotel, I didn't see Mom straight away. My stomach dropped at the empty room, though I had only been gone an hour. My eyes went instinctively to the balcony, but reason clicked in and I tapped on the bathroom door.

Are you there?

She was standing in front of the mirror, brushing her hair. One lock kept falling into her eye. She'd comb it back, press the strands in place, but the moment she let go it dropped.

I drew a bobby pin from my makeup case and fastened the curl behind her temple.

I saw Patrick's doppelgänger today, I said. Do his kids live in San Diego?

She watched me in the mirror, as if this were a test and soon I would tell her the answer. I stared back at her. Her hair was thinning around the ears, revealing patches of scalp. The folds along her upper cheek and brow had begun to close in on her eyes, as if gently guiding them to shut. Beside her, the brittle creases of my own face stretched my eyes further apart. It would be too easy to say we saw our respective pasts and futures reflected, but we shared the same basic print.

I stroked Mom's shoulder. —You hungry? Italian tonight.

I turned toward the door.

Why are you walking that way? she asked.

Just a blister.

You look like a bag lady.

Where are my bags?

Under your eyes.

I laughed. Her old self burbled up now and then.

It occurred to me, later, the intimacy of tapping on a door, asking *Are you there?* Because you expect to find them. You know who you're looking for.

This morning, I set my alarm for seven so Mom would not wake by herself. I boiled water for coffee while she sat on the balcony, where light raked across the concrete. I treasured those mornings when the sun still greeted you, when you woke and the sky told you what day it would be.

The café downstairs wouldn't open for another hour, so I boiled an egg for Mom, sliced toast soldiers.

Where's your father gone? she asked when I joined her outside. I reminded her he was living at a retirement home in Arizona.

Oh. She nodded slowly, but appeared hesitant.

You know, he's nearly ninety.

He's not.

You're getting on yourself, Mom.

She cut her eyes at me, but didn't ask. I didn't tell her.

You remember the last time I visited him in Yuma? I brought you tinned hominy and a record of *corrido* folk songs.

She breached the yolk of the egg with her toast and lifted it so slowly that a yellow tack hardened onto the crust before it reached her lip.

Our conversation continued. We shared anecdotes with each other. Mostly I shared anecdotes with her. When she finished, I cleared space on the table for the lighthouse puzzle. Oils from last night's ravioli still crumpled the tablecloth. I swept a few olive stones and shavings of parmesan to the floor and spread the puzzle between us.

Together, we turned each piece in our fingers until we recognized the notches.

The lighthouse overlooked a beach where foam sudsed over pebbles and beach glass. A bed of clams shifted with the tide. A pool gathered in the lap of a rock with mossy bunches of anemones and gunnel fish and barnacles. And all the life there.

ACKNOWLEDGEMENTS

Demi-Gods quotes Frances Leviston's "The Golden Age" and Nâzım Hikmet's "Loving You." Thank you to the authors and publishers for your permission to include these lines.

I wrote *Demi-Gods* during my PhD at the University of East Anglia. With that in mind, I'd like to thank, first of all, my supervisors Jean McNeil and Stephen Benson. Jean has probably read this novel as many times as I have: your insight has been invaluable to me. Though Stephen did not have a direct role in the novel, our conversations on rhythm seeped into my creative process. Thank you both for your support and encouragement.

I gratefully acknowledge the funding received toward my PhD from the University of East Anglia and the Social Sciences and Humanities Research Council of Canada.

Jean introduced me to Elaine Martel, a California native and sailor, who read the relevant sections and pointed out my landlubber mistakes and inconsistencies. I can't thank you enough, Elaine.

Speaking of facts and accuracy—I owe a huge thank you to the staff at the San Diego History Centre, who helped me plumb their archives so I could invoke the mood of that city and time.

Thank you, as ever, to my fearless agent Karolina Sutton, without whom none of my work would see daylight.

And thank you to my editors, Nicole Winstanley, Callie Garnett, and Alexa von Hirschberg. Especially you, Nicole, who saw a draft of this novel when it was a hot shaggy mess and didn't run away. Your commitment to me and my work means everything.

Thank you to all the witches of Ten Bell Lane, for your solidarity and magic.

Thank you Nathan Hamilton, a wonderful editor in his own right, who managed to change the course of this novel without even reading it. In all sincerity—the story found its shape in conversation with you.

Thank you, most of all, to Mom and Jesse, the most supportive family I could ask for. Particularly you, Mom, my most willing travel companion and research assistant. Thank you for your friendship and readiness.

I'm grateful to all of you.